Joy
&
Pain

Joy & Pain

FRANKLIN WHITE

STREBOR BOOKS
NEW YORK LONDON TORONTO SYDNEY

Strebor Books
P.O. Box 6505
Largo, MD 20792
http://www.streborbooks.com

ISBN 978-1-59309-217-7
ISBN 978-1-4165-7940-3 (e-book)
LCCN 2008925331

First Strebor Books trade paperback edition June 2008

Cover design: www.mariondesigns.com
Cover photograph: © Keith Saunders/Marion Designs

10 9 8 7 6 5 4 3 2 1

Manufactured in the United States of America

For information regarding special discounts for bulk purchases,
please contact Simon & Schuster Special Sales at 1-866-506-1949
or business@simonandschuster.com

The Simon & Schuster Speakers Bureau can bring authors to your
live event. For more information or to book an event, contact the
Simon & Schuster Speakers Bureau at 1-866-248-3049 or visit our
website at www.simonspeakers.com.

THIS IS FOR MESALE SOLOMON

Real friendship is deep.

ACKNOWLEDGMENTS

Thanks to all who have once again helped to make this book a reality and who gave encouragement and strength in the process. Miea, Cassandra Graves, Carl & Sue White, Richard & Ann Griffin, my entire family.

As always, thanks to Zane, Charmaine and editor Anita Diggs. Special thanks to agent Victoria Sanders. My first readers, Vanessa Woodward and Erica "E" Gordon, for keeping me on point; and Richale Thompson for the constant reminders that I have another novel in me someplace.

Proverbs has been my strength to get this book done. Thanks for the wisdom, friendship and love. I know you love me back. You make me better.

Love always to Langston, Trey and Morgan.

To the many authors who continue to succeed in their craft: Zane, Walter Mosley, Eric Jerome Dickey, Lolita Files, Kim Roby, Vickie Stringer, Margaret Hodge, Yolanda Joe, Cherlyn Michaels, Nikki Jenkins and Dr. Yvonne Sanders-Butler.

Chapter 1

I never said I wasn't a freak in the sheets for my man. Subsequently on Saturday morning, I find myself eating at the breakfast bar giving him full frontal access without regret or shame. Keith's coy smile lets me know he's pleased with the freedom of my ta-tas. So far, there's been no teasing mention of his ripped T-shirt I accidentally tore while trying to get at him after his week-long business trip to South Beach. He is feeding his face as he sits across from me in his silk pajama bottoms. We both have huge appetites; we are eating hot biscuits with molasses, eggs, and country sausage. Our hunger emerged from a romantic and non-stop Friday night, full of scented candles, warm body oils, and music by Floetry, KEM, Robin Thicke and some other sexy mood-setting, neo-soul performers I had burned just for the occasion.

I knew Keith was aware that he handled his business during the night and then some. He gave a smorgasbord of love—very satisfying in more ways than one. After six years of living together, this man can push my buttons to the limit. I can't get enough of his chocolate body and the chemistry we share.

At this point in our relationship I think we are as close as ever. Well, as close as a man ever lets a woman in his life. He talks about things that matter in his life. Asks my opinion in difficult situations and shares intimate concerns to a point that makes me feel like we are connected. Everything he is giving is fine with me. I can live and have been living with this level of commitment for a long time. I have no problem living in the moment and as time passes, I know I will get more and more because our trust is growing every day. I am sure it's been a process all through our relationship so I don't sweat it. The main thing is we are clicking, running on automatic. It is wonderful because we are definitely drama free and feeling our connection.

"You know, I could stay like this forever," Keith says to me.

I intercept his eyes, when they seize the moment to travel down the rest of my bare body when I stand to get the pot of coffee to warm our cups. I also catch his tone. It is overly campaigning for some strange reason. So I decide to check it.

"You mean, this moment? Enjoying this moment?" I confirm.

Keith looks at me quickly without explaining, then goes for more eggs and the last biscuit.

My human radar, inherited from my mother who listened to all my father's shit, up until she left him when I was ten, zooms in tightly on his response.

He is like, "Exactly, that's what I mean, baby. This right here, right now, I wouldn't change it for the world."

If being with Keith for six years has taught me anything, it is realizing unconditionally when he's shuffling me doo-doo. I reach over the table and stop his hand from stuffing more eggs into his mouth with his fork. "Don't even try it. Tell me, what you mean, Keith?"

He glances at me like he does his jurors in the high-profile divorce settlements he has a habit of winning.

"C'mon, Lala, I was just thinking how mellow it is for us right now, and I want things to stay like this, that's all."

I push. *"Like this?"*

"You know, just the two of us. It takes a huge string of luck for people to get along like this—for this long of a time period." Keith picks up his coffee cup, places his weekend special of three teaspoons of creamer down in the bottom, then begins to stir slowly and tries to dismiss my concerns. "So, you have a good time last night?" Keith is about to start patting himself on the back concerning his performance because he'd helped me to release several times through the night. He was a satisfier in the bed; almost always on a mission to please me and I loved that about him.

"Last night was okay," I let him know.

He chuckles. "Just okay?"

"That's it."

"Yeah, right."

"Would've been better, if you'd done what I asked," I say.

Keith sips his coffee. He has no expression—almost like he doesn't hear me.

"So why didn't you?"

"Lala, I keep telling you. It's like an unbreakable habit now that I pull out. It's been our practice since we've been making love without condoms."

"Keith, you're full of it. All of the grief I've gotten from you over the years about how it's so unnatural and now all of a sudden…it's an 'unbreakable habit.'"

"Grief?" He sips even more coffee and says no more.

But I can't hold back. "First of all, let's get things straight. You didn't want to practice the withdrawal method because you felt cheated, and I managed to see things your way. Then you practically begged me to get back on the pill and I gave in again. Then when I stopped taking the pill because I wanted to get my body ready for pregnancy, all of a sudden, you're now so in tune with the withdrawal method like you've never had a problem with it."

Keith looks at me over the brim of his cup. Our eyes meet and I stay glued to him without letting go. Things are becoming clear that he's been thinking of not following through with our plans. So I ask him.

"You don't want me to have your child, do you? You've changed your mind, haven't you?"

Keith doesn't say a word but he picks up another piece of sausage and shoves it in his mouth. Then he starts to chew like it is somehow a new flavor. His silence answers my question, and I need to find out why.

Chapter 2

Keith and I don't talk much for the rest of the weekend. After breakfast he goes back to bed, this time to sleep. He wakes up around five, cuts the grass, then washes his car. When he doesn't clean mine, I realize he is silently letting me know how much he does for me and how much of a *good man* he is. So, as far as he's concerned, I might as well get over my disappointment of him changing his mind about the baby.

Even though work Mondays are usually horrible in every way possible, it is really good to finally sit down and talk with my friend Adria during lunch. Girlfriends always seem to make things better when trivial nonsense is causing commotion and about to make things even worse.

"Girl…aren't you looking every bit of pregnant!" I say to Adria. At this point she is straight-up the premier poster child for "black woman with child." I begin to gently make circles with my hand around her belly, which is covered by her cotton sundress. She seems to enjoy every second of the soothing touch.

"Hello…maybe 'cause I am," she whines in frustration. "Lala, I can't wait to get this baby outta me," Adria testifies. "My feet, my back, my neck, every bone in my body is aching." She giggles but still is dead serious. To me, sister girl looks as though she is ready to explode and let the baby loose any minute.

"It won't be too long now," I remind her.

"Little over a month and at the end of this week, it's home sweet home, for seven months," Adria pushes with energy.

"Thought of a name yet?"

"I'm leaning toward Michael, but hell, I don't know. Think I'll wait until I see him. Give him something that goes with his look."

"You and your looks," I mumble. Adria is my girl but she is superficial as hell. Definitely a perfect fit for Atlanta; straight-up bourgie for no reason at all.

"So, how was the weekend?" Adria asks me.

"Terrible."

"Nothing worse than a fucked-up weekend…"

"Who're you telling? I'm the one who lived it."

"Damn, that bad?"

"It starts off fine, though…Keith comes home with a bottle of wine and shrimp from Papadoes."

"Shrimp…huh?" Adria smiles 'cause she knows the deal.

"Yes, and as usual…after he eats his shrimp, he has to eat me next."

"Craziest thing I've ever heard, but let him do his thing, girl." Adria snickers while she places her hands on her belly. "Wish someone would get up under all this ass and get a little taste," Adria confides.

"Now, that would definitely be something to talk about," I tell her.

"Anyway…," she says, with a grin on her face.

"Well, the next morning after we are still basking in the moment, Keith drops a hint that he wants things to stay the way they are…*forever*."

When Adria hears the news, her face is more confused than mine when I heard it from Keith firsthand.

"For-ever-ever?"

"That's what I'm saying. After all the promises outta his mouth about having a child when I turn thirty-three. Now, all of a sudden, he thinks there's no reason to take the next step, when I'm months from turning thirty-four."

Adria takes a deep breath and rubs her belly. "Typical cold feet, Sweetie."

At this point, I don't want to hear about any cold feet because Keith had lots of balls leading me on the way he did. And if he knows it or not, he is now interfering big time with my future and all that I have ever dreamed of. There is no question he knows what I want because we talked about getting pregnant endlessly on our cruise. We were gone six days, five nights to the islands. We had connected—at least I thought we had—and were on the same page about our plans of being together and raising a child, even if we decided against getting married at that point.

When we returned from the cruise, Keith was so adamant about a child that he accompanied me to my doctor's appointment when I decided to make sure everything was all right inside to have kids. He even brought home a crib and set it in our spare bedroom so that we would never forget our promise to each other about starting a family. There was no mistake. I was perfectly clear to him when we started dating that I was on a mission to find a man who wanted a family. When I met Keith I had already tired of the dreaded dating game. I was worn out from all the different issues and lies I had to wade and waddle through to even make sense of what a relationship could be. But Keith had seemed to be the one to take the chance with, and I did. Now I was having second thoughts but wasn't going down without a fight. I wanted to have a child with Keith like we had planned. While we waited for lunch, Adria thought she knew why Keith led me on the way he did.

"To keep peace in the house, that's how," she suggests. "You know how black men are. They would rather live a lie instead of telling us what's actually on their minds. It's something they learn from their fathers; well, the ones who even know them. The ones who don't can claim ignorance. But one thing's for sure."

"What's that?"

"Black men can't blame their single moms, because that's what I'm about to become, and we can do no wrong, you understand."

I decide to bypass Adria's train of thought and went with my own.

"I knew I should have kept my options open. I've invested over six years with this man and now, once again, he has a change of plans. It was a foolish investment, you know? I don't have one man I can call up and say, 'Look, I'm free again. Come get me and knock me up.' Maybe I'll start looking for a donor, too, maybe use the same guy that put yours in the oven."

"Girl, you don't want any parts of him. I dread the day I have to tell this child inside of me everything I know, which is very little, about the no-good bastard. Shit, maybe I won't altogether. But knowing how your man is, I bet he's banking on you coming around and seeing things his way." Adria puts her head down and mumbles before she takes a sip of her water. "Like you always do."

I tell her, "Yeah, right, that's not happening."

"You said the same thing when he wanted you to try the sex toys."

"I told you I was curious, too, and you didn't help with your sex store-shopping ass. I never asked you to buy me that rabbit or that silver bullet thing."

"Yeah, but then it was the porno films he wanted you to watch with him."

"They aren't that bad. And thanks for those, too."

"Not a problem, Sweetie. But I do seem to remember your being pissed when he expected you to cook every night, like his mother used to do for his father."

"Well, that took a little getting used to, but you gotta eat."

"Do I have to remind you the prenuptials ya'll just threw out the window at his request and after I bought my dress, no less? Now, as I understand it, ya'll don't even want to get married. His doin', no doubt, but you still rolling with his requests and decisions."

I don't have a response for Adria. She is on point at the moment.

"Then you went in on that big-ass house with him and let him put his name on the mortgage alone." Adria looks like she is enjoying telling me about me.

"Okay, okay, I get your point, damn it, with your single-mom ass. But he has to do this for me. Shit, he owes me."

"Listen to you. Men don't owe us shit but a hard time, and a hard penis from time to time. Even with papers, they don't owe us and they know it."

"He does, Adria. Every single time this man wants to change his mind about things happening in our life, I have bent over backward to appease him, no matter how I feel about the situation."

"You've spoiled him, that's for sure."

"Well, I'm not giving in on this. I've always wanted to have children, and Keith knows this, so he's just going to have to face reality."

At this moment in our conversation, I resent that Adria knows my business as much as she does. I mean, it is good that she kept me on my toes, but damn, she sure knows how to make me feel like Keith is running our relationship. After listening to her and my background sheet...I guess he is.

Chapter 3

hree weeks later, I am still at odds with Keith. We are close to roommate status. There has been no more discussion about the baby or our future, and the one time I thought about approaching him for sex I reconsidered the notion. If it was not going to be for the purpose of attempting to get me pregnant, it wasn't worth my time. So, I grabbed a toy out of my goody bag and handled my own damn business.

When my birthday rolls around, I can't explain how I feel. I am empty in a way, but damn sure happy I am alive and able to see another start of a new year of life. When I walk into work that morning, there are red and white balloons along with streamers lining my cubicle. The morning-news traffic manager is always smiling, and his grin is extra wide.

"You might be interested to know that your girl is up at Grady Hospital about to deliver that baby."

I look down at my phone to look for a message or text from Adria but nothing is there. "Are you serious?"

"Yes, and you better get over there right away; we have things covered here."

I'm at the hospital as fast as I can drive. The elevator can't seem to move fast enough for me, and my heart is racing frantically with so much joy; I am ready to see Adria and the baby. When I reach the right floor, I look in the waiting area and notice four women, all in labor but not urgently, sitting around talking with their families and watching television. I overhear a nurse mention a full moon because they'd been busy all night. Then I walk over to a board that lists new deliveries. Adria Cunningham is in room 32B.

First, I peek in on Adria, but she's sleeping. The nurse tells me she had a rough time pushing the baby out—all nine pounds and eight ounces of him. I look down at her and she is worn out, so I decide not to wake her. I'm happy that she's okay, though and I feel a smile of happiness for her; it's a new beginning.

I follow the directions to the nursery, down the hall, and through the double doors to the right. Then I'm confused but still with a smile on my face.

"Keith?" He is standing outside the nursery looking in and flinches at the sound of his name.

I walk closer to him and call out his name again, but he doesn't look at me. Keith is frozen and I am standing next to him. He still won't look at me, so I follow his eyes. He is staring into the nursery at bassinet number seven that is holding a baby boy with the name "Malcolm Cunningham" taped to it on a postcard. Seeing the baby makes me forget about Keith being there for a few seconds.

Aww…she named him Malcolm. That name is going to fit him just right…

Keith is somewhat in a daze. At this point, this is good for me because I'm glad he can actually see what we could share together. But I'm still confused. "So, what are you doing here?"

"Adria called the house so I came over."

"Oh, so—why didn't you call me?"

"'Cause I wanted to be the first to see my child."

Keith has offered some pretty corny jokes before, so I blew this one off, like I do all the others.

"No, seriously, why didn't you call me when Adria called the house?"

Finally, Keith looks me square in the eyes. "He's mine, Lala. The baby's mine."

Chapter 4

I smack Keith's face and walk away from him quickly without a word. My body is feeling like it's going to erupt; let go like the worst boiling point ever imagined. Misplaced is how I feel. Misguided is how I try to quickly understand the reality of it all. Thoughts running at warp speed. My fuckin' body has lightning bolts stinging it, and at this moment, I am losing my mind. I hear Keith call out to me, but I'm walking away or my next stop is jail. There's nothing he can say to me. I wait for the elevator for a few seconds, then decide to bolt down the stairwell to the garage.

When I get to the garage, I'm crying puddles and winded. Anger, deceit—all that shit is crawling up in me. My hands are shaking and I can't find my car. I drop my keys and when I pick them up, my eyes spot Keith's car which is right in front of me. I don't think twice. I find his key on my ring and jump in that motherfucker without blinking.

As soon as I sit down and try to put the key in the ignition, for the first time, I hate the smell of his car.

Finally, I start his car. I hate his fuckin' smooth-ass jazz playing, too. I wipe my eyes the best way I can before I pull out.

After they are clear, I can see that he has already packed his belongings and has what could fit in the backseat. I fight like hell not to start crying again. The car feels cold to me—just like the unworthy son-of-a-bitch Keith. I'm collected as much as I can be, so I ease out the parking space. As I put the car in drive, I look up into the windshield. Keith appears and steps in front of the car about ten feet away like he's the mighty King Kong.

He yells, "L..." He has the nerve to call me the pet name he uses with me in bed.

I place my foot on the brake and try my best to remember how to roll down the driver's side window but I'm flustered and sure 'nuff nervous so I can't. I smash the button over and over that peels back his sunroof over his cries to be careful in his punk-ass BMW 740. I scream, "Nigga, don't you ever call me 'L' again. Do you understand!"

He places his left hand in his suit pants, then motions with his right for me to relax.

"Okay, I understand, but you have my car, Lala. I need my car."

"Well, you had my soul and burnt it. So we're even."

"Look, Lala, I'm sorry, okay?"

"'Sorry'?" At this point I'm so mad, I'm standing on

his seat looking at this fool with my head out his sun-roof.

"Yes, I am. And we don't have to do this like this, Lala. We can talk later, okay, but right now, I need my car."

A man passes by and he wants to know if I'm okay. Keith tells him everything is fine then tells him to step the fuck off, when he slows to see what is going on.

I'm sitting behind the wheel again and Keith's arro-gance lights the wick that makes me want to do some-thing drastic. Something he will never forget. Cause his ass some pain, something like cutting off his dick and sticking it up his ass.

"Lala, for the last time, I need my car!" Keith shouts at me like if I don't, it is going to be the worst mistake of my life.

"You say you need your car, motherfucker?"

He exhales. "Yes, I need to get to work. I have a major case in twenty minutes."

The arrogant bastard really believes that I give a good fuck about his case when I just found out that he's made a baby with my friend. All the time, it is about his cases, his job, and his future. He tugs at his tie a few times and looks as though he's trying to get himself ready for court.

"Well, I have a case, too. A case of the ass!" And with-out warning I slam his car into gear and place my foot hard on the gas as though it's stuck in cement. He's so busy primping that he doesn't even see me coming.

"Lala!" is all I hear over Keith's roaring engine right

before he turns around and starts placing his Kenneth Coles to pavement, one after the other, as quickly as he possibly can. I am trying to definitely run his black ass over. "Lala! Lala, please…," he pleads over and over again while I'm inching closer and closer to his backside.

Keith probably didn't know he could run so fast. His knees are high and the sound of his screaming voice, only makes me more upset. All the while as I'm driving and chasing him down, I'm screaming, too, thinking how he must have thought he was the biggest player in Atlanta while he fucked two good friends at the same time. For what reason, I don't know, but all of a sudden, Keith stops running and I swear, I have no intentions of letting up on the gas. I just don't care.

"Lala!" he wails, looking at me through his windshield with his terrified expression. Keith's not so all that now. No cockiness or self-assured smirks. My reflexes of seeing him having flashbacks of his tired and worthless life, direct me to slam on the brakes. Tires screech, then produce smoke, and finally the car stops inches from his knee caps. In an instant, he jumps on the hood of the car just before I cripple his ass for the remainder of his natural-born life. He's looking at me through the windshield now. Sweating profusely, breathing heavily, and his eyes are close to letting go all the tears that are welling up.

"Why the tears, Keith?" I just had to know. How could someone so bold be so damn petrified when they get caught up in their deceit?

He yells into the car. "Because damn it, you're trying to kill me out here, that's why!"

"Who said I was trying to kill you, Keith?"

"You don't have to say shit. It's all in your actions."

"Maybe I *should* kill you."

"Look, Lala…"

"Just shut up and tell my why, Keith?"

He has a blank expression on his face.

"Tell me why, or we're goin' for a little ride, Playboy…"

"Lala, what the fuck are you talking about?" I see Keith look to the ground. He's thinking about jumping off.

"I'm going to ask you one more time. Why?"

"Why what?"

I don't feel like Keith's bullshit. How can he not know what I'm asking him?

His car is still in gear, so I punch it again. The speed of the car snaps back his head, and his eyes bulge out even wider as though they are seconds from popping out of his cranium. Keith screams, like it's his first night in jail, when he feels the car tilt down and around the berm; I'm driving as fast as I can under the conditions. The winding downhill path to the exit never seems to end, and I can care less if Keith continues to hold on or not. When I get to the end of the decline, I slam on the brakes and listen to Keith yell. He is now airborne and saying his prayers to the man above.

I scatter to grab whatever money I can find in my purse and give it to the attendant who is wondering what the hell is going on. Keith licks his wounds and tries to get up off the pavement. The attendant lifts the bar and I slowly go through, then stop and get out of the car and look over at Keith.

"Lala…" Keith struggles to his feet.

"You want to tell me now?" I holler back.

"Look, Lala, I'm sorry, okay. I fucked up. Just listen to me."

It is my turn to wipe away my own tears. I would have never guessed my man was stepping out on me, making a child. I know the pain is just starting. "No, Keith. I can't listen to you," I tell him. Then I get back in his car and drive away without looking back.

Chapter 5

I drive Keith's car to Lenox Mall, park in a parking lot that charges twenty dollars an hour, then take a cab home. At the moment I don't know what else to do. Reality is setting in fast and the idea of Keith and Adria in the bed having sex, not to mention their baby, is so distasteful and disrespectful. A straight-up kick in the face. My mind is unorganized and glazed over. It is my first time being involved in something so foul since my mother confronted my father about making love to her and his ho on the other side of town on the same day. But I was a young girl then. It didn't really concern me, 'cause I didn't really understand it. But this situation does. I am feeling like no one in the world has experienced what I'm feeling. It is a blurry, fucking dream; an unbreakable, terrifying trance spinning minute by minute without pause. Just the thought of Keith and Adria making a child together is enough to take all the air out of my balloon. There is no other way to explain it. I am simply flat-out *crushed*.

Keith's reaction on his face while he looked at that

baby was the icing on the cake. He was actually melting. All cooing and loving and shit. *What the fuck is wrong with me, for him to want to make a baby with Adria?* is just one of many questions rambling through my mind. Then I somehow fight through all the other bullshit like how they must have confided in each other during pillow talk; at least trusted each other to some level. Through all the time I'd spent with both of them, there was never any reason to believe they had been running around behind my back.

Something definitely had to be wrong with me; my mind wouldn't let go. For my man, and supposedly best friend, to do this to me, either I wasn't a good woman or a good friend. I had been assassinated and didn't like it one bit.

I probably cried for three straight days. No television. No radio. Complete silence. Only thoughts of what was. If my mother hadn't been dead, I would have called her and let her tell me that I was a fool for letting Keith string me out for six years without any papers, even though things seemed to be fine just the way they were. I hadn't thought about my father who'd been missing in action for years and who probably hadn't missed a night's sleep thinking about me. But I wondered how he would react…if he would come and save his baby girl, at least tell me why men were so fucked up and uncaring.

I hated being up in the house alone. Everything reminded me of Keith and his lying ass. His favorite chair. The plasma hanging on the wall that he liked to watch Judge Hatchett on. His ugly paintings he bought off eBay from some painter in Romania. I can't believe he left in my possession his entire collection of signed James Baldwin novels.

When he calls to ask about his car, I tell him I am moving out as soon as possible. He has the nerve to promise he will give me my money back that I put on the house and tells me to take my time moving. That's when I hang up on him because I can't stand to hear him act like he has cared anything about my well-being. Being isolated makes me replay our entire relationship in my mind. Meeting him, the chase, the clumsy first-time kiss, our plans and future. During this moment, I still need to figure out where I went wrong—so wrong to make my man go and sleep with my friend. This is just one part of the equation because my friend also played a major role in how I am feeling and the predicament I'm in. Usually when you're mad at your man, you can talk to your girlfriend. Or if you're upset with your girlfriend, you could at least blow off steam to your man. I'm in a web because I don't have a soul to talk to, and I need to vent about two people who have been a major part of my life for years.

I just can't take it anymore. I have to get out of the

house, plus my body needs some nourishment. I decide to go get a bite to eat and nibble at the buffet at Ryan's. Afterward, I drive around town, and on the way home, I spot a bar. Without even thinking about what type of place it is, or who might be lurking inside, I go in to order a drink.

It is dark inside. Candlelit with most of the candles minutes from being depleted. There is just enough room for people to drown their sorrows but not enough to dance on the floor behind me. A few patrons are sitting close at the few small, aged, wooden tables placed on the dark hardwood floor. Others are spaced out at the bar, far enough away from one another so the closest person next to them can't hear them mumbling to themselves about their own forsaken problems.

I sit at the bar—for me a big step because I don't do things so arbitrarily. I like to be in a safe place that I'm familiar with. This dark pub no doubt has history. Looking around, I would guess a few murders have gone down inside over the years. The physical bar where I take a seat looks like the dark redwood has been polished every night after closing and once again before the bar opens. There are at least three chairs separating me from the next person on the right and two spaces on the left. It is so dark that everyone looks like silhouettes. This is fine. I just want to mellow out and hopefully let this be a first step of letting go of everything that has happened. Keith. Adria. Their baby.

I order a Sea Breeze and before I realize it, the bartender asks if I want my third one. I tell him yes and seconds later, an image appears from the corner of the bar. As it gets closer, it turns into a face. I don't particularly want to look but I know it is a man. He sits down next to me. I glance at him long enough to tell he is an older black man, before I make sure my legs are completely under the bar and my purse with car keys sitting snugly on my lap. The bartender brings my drink and nods at the man sitting next to me.

"Cognac neat," he says. His voice is deep but polite.

I give him another quick glance. My buzz takes over my thoughts and I open my mouth. "What is that, a world-renowned playboy drink or something?"

I feel the man look at me. He doesn't answer. He watches the bartender pour his drink, then lights up this cigar that has the aroma of chocolate. It's actually quite nice, especially for me, because I hate smoke. I only asked the question because it was a reminder of Keith who would always order the same drink when we'd go out.

The bartender comes back, looks around, then pulls an ashtray from under the bar and sets it down.

"I know I'm not supposed to smoke in here. But hey, who's gonna find out?" he says without directly looking at me. He places his cigar into the ashtray and picks up his drink like it is such a delight.

"Jesus, do all men think like that?" I don't look at him, either.

"Excuse me?"

I don't answer him. I do take another sip of my drink though. About a minute later, I say to him as he puffs away on his cigar, "What if you do get caught? Then what?"

He turns on his stool to face me. "Well, I'll just have to deal with the consequences." Right then, I feel his eyes finally travel me head to toe.

"Whatever shall be, will be."

I finally turn completely toward him. I was right. He is older. My first thought is that he's the type of man that you didn't want to cross with his Delroy Lindo-looking ass. He's slick-looking but very dignified. He's darker than my father, and that's saying something. I notice his salt-and-pepper beard. I watch him pick up his cigar again and his movements are not wasted, yet very smooth. His shirt displays a top-of-the-line quality like in the pages of *GQ* that fits him perfectly. I spot a stunning watch on his wrist that goes perfectly with his gritty mystique. I don't let his presence intimidate me, though.

Too much time has expired to speak again on my comment but I do, anyway. "No matter who's affected, right?"

He recalls the few words between us "Oh, I didn't say that." He puts his cigar down, then points to it. "If the smoke bothers you, I'll gladly relinquish it." He kind of smiles and shakes his head at the same time. Then he reaches out his hand. "Hi, I'm Sydney. Sydney Patterson."

"Lala Paige," I tell him.

"Forgive me, if I'm wrong. But I'm getting the vibe that someone's done you wrong."

"Oh, you think?"

"Yes, I do."

"Well, Sydney, you're absolutely right because I don't normally walk into strange places, start drinking, let alone talk to strangers."

Sydney orders another round. By now, it is close to three in the morning and we are the only customers in the entire establishment. Sydney hasn't told me what he does professionally yet…but I have a pretty good idea he knows some pretty shady people.

We have been interrupted at least three times, by two different men who have had the urge to whisper something in Sydney's ear. After the first guy appears, a big black man about three hundred and sixty pounds with the confidence to wear a yellow pinstriped suit, walks in and mumbles something to Sydney that takes exactly two seconds. I'm feeling uncomfortable now and just about ready to get in my car and go. But Sydney apologizes for the interruptions and promises the guys are no problem at all…in fact his friends. So I stay but I am very cautious of their return. I admit, it feels good having a conversation with someone who absolutely means nothing to me. No one has to tell me I am tipsy. Sydney has sat patiently and let me tell him how I have wasted the last six years of my life and to boot, the last week. He is a good listener and I like that.

Sydney is shocked, too, when I tell him about the baby. He doesn't pass judgment but lets me know he thinks the whole situation is definitely bullshit—and not a situation someone as sweet as me should have to go through.

It's time for me to leave. Sydney walks me outside but we just stand by the entrance facing the quiet street. A few minutes later the bartender walks out, shuts the door behind him, then locks the place up and wishes us a good night.

Sydney looks good under the city lights. He tells me I do, too. There's no doubt he's had his share of ladies because he's just that smooth. Polite. Caring. Sensitive. I swear I hadn't thought about what I do next until the moment, but I reach out to kiss Sydney. He doesn't resist and there we are in each other's arms going at it like we never have done it before, and I don't care one bit. I really enjoy the way Sydney kisses me. He tastes so good and smells like he has been lightly dipped in Armani Code. The way he presses against my lips is simple but very effective. It's like he knows his conversation has already impressed me, and the kiss is the icing on the cake. He doesn't take what I am giving him for granted and respects what I'm offering. When he begins to change the pressure of his lips by easing back and forth, all the while running his fingers in my hair directly over my ear, I begin to melt. I want more. I don't care. I want more because at that moment I feel he understands me. I become bold, then stop kissing when I realize he would very well be worth the try. He'd just help me to begin to forget everything happening to me.

I touch him. "Damn, Sydney."

"Problem?" He has a grin on his face.

"Yes, a nice-sized one…But a problem I don't mind."

"Yeah, and it's all natural. No Viagra here."

We both share a laugh. This time he makes the first move for the kiss. I can't explain it, but my head starts to spin, running with wild and crazy thoughts that I don't want to suppress. Sydney has worked his hands inside my shirt. It surprises me because I didn't even realize he'd unbuttoned it. He can't place his entire hand through the space he creates, but his fingertips feel just fine as they first massage, then begin pulling at my nipple. *How does he know it was my spot?* I start to kiss him harder when I realize I am extremely moist and definitely ready for what he has to give. I am full of rage, revenge and lust; to put it mildly *all fucked up* and want to act on my feelings, not caring one bit about the consequences. I want to take Sydney by his hand and go someplace for days and lie on my back until I feel all my problems are gone.

I stop kissing.

"So, what's next?" I need to know.

"You tell me?" Sydney says.

"I want you. I want you to take me someplace, any place, do whatever you like."

"Lala…"

"I'm serious. Sydney, you're just what I need right now."

He kisses me again. I could have done it right then and there.

"I can't, sweetheart," he says.

"Why not?"

"Just isn't my style. Yes, I could take you, but afterward would you be happy with yourself?"

I am about to answer, but he places his finger over my lips.

"No, you wouldn't. My conversation with you tells me that. I don't want to take advantage of you; a friend would never do that. Besides, you've been through too much as it is."

I try again to change Sydney's mind. I kiss him some more. Tug at him and touch his firmness with my hand. I even open my shirt and guide his hands on my breasts urging him to pull at my nipples. But he's relentless with his decision. Never looks down at me, though; he knows I need this moment. He remains a gentleman. Sydney doesn't let me drive home. We sit in his car talking and listening to jazz until a cab comes to pick me up. When I wake up the next morning, I find his number in the pocket of my jacket.

Chapter 6

I call into work and take another sick day. This one makes four. I knew the station was hurting with me and Adria out, but believe me...they didn't want me there because a sister had a headline for they ass. I did feel good that Sydney saw right through me and didn't take advantage. I was somewhat embarrassed, looking back to how I behaved, but he didn't make me feel embarrassed. I enjoyed that.

Yet, this morning my sexual urge still hasn't dissipated. So, I go to my goody bag and take out the toys that Adria had bought me when I told her about Keith's request to bring them into our bed. After I finish, I sleep the rest of the morning away. When I awake I take the box of toys and throw them in the trash and promise myself I am closing shop forever. No man will ever be worthy of my loving again because it just isn't worth the trouble. If I need relief again, the urge is going to have to take care of itself.

I do a lot of soul searching that day. I need to change. Get better. Feel better. So, I decide that I am going to get back in the gym. For me, no matter what stage in my life, it seems as though when my body is in top shape, things run smoother and I am able to deal with whatever comes my way quickly and decisively. I take a cab back to the bar to get my car, then drive to the gym. When I arrive, I decide that I want to make my body sweat so I jump on a treadmill. Close to three miles into my workout, I begin to think about some of the things Sydney and I had discussed.

Sydney was an interesting man when it came to relationships. I gathered he knew so much because he had been blessed to live and understand what he had actually experienced himself. He understood that pain from relationships was awful, and I was grateful that he did. While we sat and talked I don't know how many times I complained about my situation. But he understood and didn't look at me like I was some whiny bitch who couldn't believe her fine ass could be cheated on. I came to realize his knowledge about women wasn't from things he had heard in over his fifty years of living but actually *what he* had lived. He understood my embarrassment and the surprise of my situation. The entire night Sydney never gave me a reason why men do some of the doggish things they do to women. He did tell me that he had done his share that probably made his mother turn over in her grave. He said it had a lot to do with growing up and knowing himself as a man. Sydney let me know that he never knew his father. The only examples he was able to be around were his uncles who all drove Cadillacs and did unspeakable things to women that were in their lives. But Sydney did force me to look into my own life.

One of the things he asked me that stuck out was if I had a problem with choosing men who didn't have a good track record with women. Keith always told me that the women he dated all dumped him for some reason or another. There was his college sweetheart who, after graduation, decided that she wanted to experiment with her sexuality and be "friends" with the roommate she'd had during her four years. This blew his mind. Then there was the one who decided that her career was too important to her to be locked into a relationship.

I was honest with Sydney and told him Keith had been the first man that I'd let in. I wasn't a virgin or anything, but mentally, he was the first man ever, besides my father, whom I had let into my life. I was happy to give in to him this way because it let me know that I really cared about him. When Sydney asked if I thought Keith respected me before any of this started to happen, I had to give his question some thought. I remembered there had been times when Keith would become upset with me because I didn't see his point of view or I didn't want to do things the way he did. Like buy the house together without both of our names on the mortgage which probably was a big mistake because he was now gone. I felt that he respected me. But I was beginning to think that the amount of time that we'd spent together was part of the reason he disrespected me with Adria the way he did. We hardly ever took any time away.

I try to keep an open mind during my workout, but being introspective about what has happened is not happening for me. It is way too early to decide why everything turned out this way—there are too many questions that I don't have answers to. While I do my last set of lunges, they sting like hell. I decide there is no way in hell I am going to figure out why Keith has done this to me by guessing. I realize that I need to know—to be able to move on with my life, so I decide to find out where Keith is and ask him myself.

Chapter 7

I end up calling Keith's friend Alex to find out where he is. If anyone knows his whereabouts Alex will. I had met him through Keith and always had been on the fence with him. At times, I would feel he'd tell Keith things to persuade him that his so-called committed relationship was something he really didn't want to do. When I would see Alex, I would always give him shit when he would visit and brag about all the girls he dated; how he would never settle down. He'd known Keith a long time and were boys in every sense of the word.

In the beginning of our conversation, he is distant but his weasel eyes tell me he knows things. He is being deliberately careful about what he divulges. I can tell Keith has filled him in on what is happening with us because he is straight up talking in pieces. After my constant barrage of questions, Alex slips up. He lets it be known that Keith has a new place in Buckhead. So, I go to pay him a visit.

❖❖❖

I follow the directions Alex gave. It takes me around twenty minutes to drive. It's an upscale condominium subdivision off Peachtree. There looks to be at least three-hundred units and there is a sign boasting an *all-adult community*. I drive around for a few minutes, then I notice Keith's car and I park right beside it. As usual, his car is waxed and sparkling clean. I notice a long scratch, more like a deep scrape, on the front bumper from our incident in the parking garage. Oh well.

I walk up to the door, then knock. As if he is expecting me, Keith opens the door without saying a word.

"Alex told you I was coming, didn't he?"

He says, "What're friends for?"

"Same thing I want to ask Adria," I tell him.

"Look, Lala, don't make a scene." Keith looks behind me to see if anyone is around. "This time, I'll call the police and I'm dead serious."

I pause for a moment and look at Keith. It doesn't seem like he has missed me one bit. He looks like he just finished working out and he has a glass of water in his hand.

"I just came to talk."

"About?"

I kind of laugh at him. "Can I come inside, Keith?"

"I'm warning you, Lala…"

"There's nothing to worry about, okay?"

He glances at me up and down. Trying to read a sista. Keith opens the door wider and looks down at me as I walk past. I make it a special point to look good. Let him see what he lost out on. My nails, hair, toes, along with my outfit, are definitely all working nicely together.

I walk down the hallway a few steps on the way, passing a few rooms. Then there's this breathtaking sunken living room fully furnished.

"I didn't know these were furnished."

He says, "They're not."

"How'd you get all of this so quickly then?"

Keith takes a hard deep breath. "Lala, I've had this place for the last five months."

I am real close to blowing up at Keith's confession. I fight back the thousands of questions that pop into my head. I feel emotion straining my eyes. Powerful. Painful. I feel myself squinting and do an unbelievable three-hundred-and-sixty-degree turn looking at his place. *Not a penny less than four-hundred thousand dollars*, I think to myself.

I step down into the sunken sitting space and sit in a contemporary-style chair. This is when I realize his betrayal was planned to a certain point. Keith is smart enough not to get too close to me; he remains in the hall looking down into the sitting room.

He runs his hand across the maple wood banister. "So, is there something you want to talk about?"

I'm thinking, *Uh…yeah? You dirty motherfucker. What the hell is going on? I can't believe this shit! You're a lying-ass used tampon.* But I stay focused enough not to let my anger spike through. So, I instead say, "I just have a few questions."

"Okay, let's hear it."

"I just want to know what happened to us?"

Keith starts to walk down and sit close to me. But he gives me a second look and sits on the steps leading to where I am, far enough away where I can not jump at him.

"Lala, it's hard to explain."

"How so?"

"First of all, I didn't want it to happen like this."

I open my arms to his new place. "Looks like you had everything under control to me."

"I'm saying...I just didn't know how to tell you."

"What? Tell me you were leaving or that you got Adria pregnant?"

"Both."

"Which happened first?"

Keith thinks about his answer.

"Lala, I've been thinking about a change for years."

It is hard for me to take what he is saying. "Years?"

Keith rushes his answer. Nervously. "At least two."

"Two years, Keith? You never said anything about being unhappy with me or wanting to leave. We discussed our future together. I mean, hell, we just bought the house."

"Lala, maybe you want yourself to believe that, but for a while I would say it every day and all you'd tell me was, '*I didn't mean what I was saying*.' But I did mean it. I really did. The house, shit, it was a mistake, but I'll continue to make my half of my share of the mortgage for as long as you want to stay there."

"Keith, how are you going to do that? Where is all the extra money coming from?"

He smiles. "I made partner, Lala, and I am a fifty-fifty owner of the new hip-hop station that starts on the air next month."

"Partner...radio station?"

"Made partner three months ago and worked the deal for the station almost a year ago now."

"And you didn't tell me?"

"I just didn't know how to approach you with any of this. Especially knowing where it was headed."

"So, the last few years of being together were just wasted time?"

"Basically," Keith says. His voice is so matter-of-fact. "I just lost interest."

"So, that's how Adria came into the picture?"

"Adria?"

"Yes, the mother of your child."

"She's kind of difficult to explain."

"Not as much as she is to accept."

"I don't know where to start."

"Why don't you start when you started to fuck her?"

"Really?"

"Yeah, why not, Keith. I want to hear about the first

time you decided to betray my trust all the way to where you bust a nut in her and get her pregnant."

"I'm not going to be so graphic, Lala."

"Why not? You never wanted to cum inside *me* for whatever reason."

We both thought about what we were saying to each other.

"Look, Lala. Adria, always from the day I met her, flirted with me."

"I didn't know that. Why didn't you tell me?"

"Why bother? It's something that just goes with the territory living in Atlanta...you know how it is."

"No, I don't. So, tell me."

"She just started to show up everywhere."

"What do you mean 'everywhere'?"

"To start with—down at the club at happy hour, when I was talking shop with my coworkers."

"So? Her showing up means she gets pregnant by you?"

"Listen to me. She would come in. I didn't want to disrespect her by not acknowledging her presence. So, one night we talked and from there things just took off."

"For how long, Keith.?"

"How long?"

"Yes, how long did the two of you sneak behind my back?"

"About a year and a half."

I feel the first tear fall down my face. All of the pain that I felt when I found out about the baby has returned. It's multiplied by a hundred-fold.

"Damn, Lala, c'mon, please stop crying." Keith asks at least three times. I'm not going to lie, I do try to stop. I don't enjoy letting Keith see me this way. I don't want him to see how much he has hurt me, but I can't control all the shit that's coming out of me. After a while, I am sobbing like a baby…going over everything he ever promised me and our relationship.

"I know, Lala, I fucked up. This, I know," Keith tells me. He is now kneeling beside me holding my hand.

"Keith, I didn't expect this type of shit from you! Never would I have imagined you would do me this way. If someone had done your sister this way, you'd be ready to kick somebody's ass."

All Keith can do is repeat my name over and over again. There is nothing else he can do to comfort me. He doesn't have an excuse for what he has done. I continue to ask why but his "losing interest" excuse doesn't work. I snatch my hand from him and start to swing at him. I don't get a chance to hit him hard enough to make him understand the pain he has caused. When he grabs my arms and pins them down to my side, I hate to admit this man has power over me.

After twenty to thirty minutes of tussling, we end up in Keith's bed. I do remember him asking me to stop crying and trying to wipe the tears from my eyes. Keith says he doesn't like seeing me this way. His words give me comfort…as much as they can since he is the idiot who actually caused my pain. My mind is analyzing the shit he whispers, and in a weird sort of way, I become soothed that he cares. But that doesn't make me stop crying. I am bawling without fail. When he takes my face into his hand and turns it toward his own, that's when the moment starts to change. He presses his lips onto mine with the type of combining force that is erotic, raw, uncontrolled passion. As he kisses me, I allow him to work his tongue in my mouth. Our kiss turns into an animalistic urge that tells my mind that I want Keith to fuck me, like never before.

We are panting hard. "Shit, I'm so sorry, Lala." Keith kisses me some more.

I start to kiss him back but even harder. "I can't fuckin' stand you for putting me through this," I tell him.

I tear his shirt and he looks at me like he remembers the last time I did. I take my own clothes off for him, and he pays long attention to my nipples and gives the pleasure I need.

For the first time in my life, I feel like what has happened to me was no one's fault but my own. This is the way I should have fucked him in the first place, then this situation would have never happened. Ever since the day we had been separated, I had subconsciously thought all this was my fault. *I put too much pressure on him to give me a baby and didn't understand, nor could see that he had become bored with what I was giving him.* I think. I open my legs wide for Keith when I feel his tongue tracing my stomach. Much wider than I'd ever had before. I call him a bastard when he finally licks my spot, then I grab his head and pull it up and instruct him to stick out his tongue so I can see it. I shout down at him to make it firm. I have never done anything like this, but I remember that it was one of Adria's favorite tricks that she loved to brag about after a night of humping with one of her friends, maybe even Keith.

Anger seeps through my emotions because the bitch could have told me she had been using my man. When I push Keith's tongue back inside, I make sure he touches every wall. I pull Keith's face back up, then haul off and smack him. He grunts but I could care less, then I smack his ass again. I want him to feel my pain. We stay in the bed for the rest of the night, and our rage turns into lovemaking around three in the morning as we listen to the "Quiet Storm." We talk again, make love, then talk some more. By the time I reach my car in the morning, Keith and I have made up.

Chapter 8

Later that night, I'm back at the bar with Sydney. After I spill my guts, he places his shot glass down on the bar and I am kind of surprised by the clunk it makes.

"Didn't mean to scare you, but hell, you're killing me. Did you say, your man?"

"I'm kind of throwing the idea around."

"Lala…"

"You think I'm moving a bit too fast, don't you? Don't look at me like I don't have a clue, Sydney."

Sydney points to the bartender for another and wipes his mouth slowly with a napkin. Then I notice him lick his lips. "Hella fast. Some cyber, optimized DSL shit. Geez, it was just one night."

"But he's sorry. I truly felt it."

"Trust me, the boy *is* sorry for what he's done to you. Men always regret our dirt after we're caught. I never said we aren't caring souls…but it's always after we get caught." Sydney smiles and waves very cool at a few people as they come in the bar. "Look, you're confused and he confused you some more."

"Maybe."

"And you're still upset."

Sydney was right. Mad about how our history together should have kept him away from Adria. All the time we spent together made me want to forget about his baby and Adria and get along with our lives. At one point, I even wondered how much he would have to pay for child support while he stayed with me.

Sydney reads my face.

"Confused, right…"

I tell him I am, then smile.

We pause for a minute so the bartender can give him another shot and me a Long Island Iced Tea.

"Take your time, no need to rush into anything," he continues.

"It will probably be a lot of work but just maybe we can patch things up."

"Hunny, trust me, this isn't a patch job. You try to patch this up and soon enough, you're looking at a bigger tear, down the road."

I look away from Sydney for a moment and up toward the small speakers perched on some nicely varnished shelves. "Is that 'Happy Feelings' by Frankie Beverly?"

Sydney is lighting up a smoke. As usual he is dressed to the nines and his cologne is magnificent. "One and only."

"I love his music!"

Sydney chuckles a bit. "When Chuck gets the urge to

play music inside this joint, that's the only damn song you'll ever hear in here."

"That's fine with me, 'cause it doesn't get any better than Frankie. He is the only musician I know who can pack a concert hall on a consistent basis and hasn't had an album in years."

"Talking about a brother who deserves a lifetime achievement award…"

"Umm, hmm."

"Look, there's nothing wrong with wanting to save your relationship. Trust me, I know. Six years is a long investment for anyone to let go of without taking a second look at it."

"I can't refuse my love for this man, can I? 'Cause I do still love him."

"Understood, but love is deeper than love."

Sydney's words puts us in one of those moments where I feel like he is the teacher and I his student. It is probably the reason I enjoy talking to him. I value his opinion. He never pushes it on me. I had spoken to him over the phone more times than I could count since we met. I'd never known a man so able to listen to a woman's crazy happenings in life about another man and be truly interested.

I knew my share about him as well. Sydney was married but in an open relationship with his wife. It took some time for me to understand the premise of "OPEN," but he explained it as a complete agreement with his wife that they'd been dealing with for a while. I never saw a ring on his finger—not that it means much these days—and I don't know how I would have felt if I would have slept with him the night he had me sprung. But I did admire that they had the guts to be so proactive and honest when it came to their relationship after being together for so long.

They married young—he was twenty-two, she was nineteen, and they had been together for the past thirty-two years. An accomplishment within itself. Sydney had his own place where he would spend time a few days a week. I got the impression that he enjoyed a really good conversation rather than anything else, especially after he passed on having sex with me. He told me the only guideline in their open marriage was the promise to never hurt each other beyond repair. I took that as meaning never to get too involved with anyone who would jeopardize all the years they had invested in each other.

I can't figure out what Sydney means concerning "love is love," and he begins to explain.

"Look, understand this. There is love and there is *love*."

"O…kay," I say to him still not understanding.

"It's like this. The love that we covet is much more shallow than what love really is."

"Tell me about it."

"We're conditioned by society that love is somewhere out here for us. All of us. So we go on this big love hunt, looking for someone to fulfill our needs which we don't fully understand ourselves because we change our minds so much."

"Been there, too."

"So, once we find someone who qualifies as what we are looking for, we push ourselves to love them, even if we don't feel a spiritual connection to them. You see, when I met my wife, the very first time I saw her, there was a connection and I knew that I would make her my wife. It was a connection that was spiritual, not lustful. There was no question about it that I wanted to be with her."

"So, did you ever have problems?"

"Who doesn't? But with any problem, it's never gotten to a point where we don't think we won't be together. And not once in all our years of being totally exclusive and totally committed have I strayed."

"So, this whole open thing with her. How'd that come along?"

"It was her idea. I don't know how long it will last, but we all need a break from time to time. Shit, we've been together so long I don't even want to know another woman like I know her."

"That deep, huh?"

"Deeper."

"What about sleeping with others? How's that work?"

"Well, if she does, she has the option to tell me or not to. It's her decision."

"So has she?"

"Don't know."

"Have you?"

"No, but I've come awfully close." Sydney begins to laugh.

Our conversation is good. I actually thought we were going to have a drink, then go for something to eat. I am surprised when Chuck comes out with our meal. Barbecue ribs, coleslaw, collard greens, candied yams and for dessert, New York-style cheesecake.

We eat and talk some more.

"You have a sister up in here embarrassing herself."

"Yeah, Chuck, he's special. Man can burn, not many like him. I've known him for over twenty years. He was the head chef for my restaurant."

"Really, you were a restaurateur?"

"Absolutely. In the early eighties, down on Peachtree, one of the first black restaurants to turn a profit in Atlanta."

"Wow, that's big-time."

"Yeah, it was a good time."

"You miss it?"

"It was good while it lasted. I met a lot of good people with a lot of good stories."

"So, what is it you do now?"

Sydney's voice is stern. "Solve problems."

"Sydney…"

"Really, I solve problems and situations that may be dwelling in your mental space."

"What are you talking about?"

"Like I said, you have a problem. Come to me."

I laugh him off. "I'll certainly keep that in mind."

Sydney looks up from his plate. From his stare I know it is important.

"Since you're thinking about taking him back, let me make a suggestion."

"What's that?"

He takes a healthy sip of his drink, then says, "Go see the mother of his child."

Chapter 9

I don't take Sydney's advice right away. A sit-down with a skank? Uh, uh, no way, no fuckin' how. Adria was not only the mother of Keith's child but the foul tramp who took my friendship and disrespected me like no one ever had before. It was bad enough that I had to deal with the constant thoughts of her making love to my man and sharing him with her. But Sydney didn't let up on his cajoling. As a matter of fact, after a few phone calls, days later, he had all but convinced me to go see her. I kind of understood that I would have to face her sooner or later. Sydney's point was, we were going to have to work together and our place of employment definitely was not the best place to finally see each other after all that had happened.

So, I decide to go. I don't tell Keith about my plans to see Adria. At this point, I have been over to his place on two separate occasions, spending the night both times.

We had dinner once and lots of phone calls in between as we tried to patch things back together. Maybe talking with Adria would soothe my mind about Keith's explanation that what they had was only a physical fling and was completely over.

I ring Adria's doorbell on a Tuesday and I look at my watch; it's seventeen minutes past twelve. When she opens the door to her townhouse, she is holding the baby and I can tell he's wearing her ass out. She looks drowsy, sleep deprived and on edge. Serves her right; if I would have been there under girlfriend circumstances, I would have told her to give me that baby and go get some sleep.

I can tell without a blood test that the baby is Keith's. Same color, same eyes. He has a little coconut head, a gift from mother, but a full head of hair. His eyes are closed and he is snuggled up tight to Adria's neck. Adria doesn't hide her embarrassment at holding my man's child. She drops her head and stiffens a bit, waiting on my reaction. But what was I going to do? Slap the shit out of her while she was holding the little one?

"Hi, Adria," is all I can say. I try not to sound like the sight of her holding the baby isn't cutting my insides wide open.

She tries a fake smile, but I can tell she has been waiting for my visit. "Lala!" Her tone is even more ridiculous. It's laced with shame and guilt, but I get past it the best way I can by trying to ignore it and play my own game.

"Hey, girl, I just stopped over to see how you're doing." I follow Adria's eyes as they drop to my hands to see if I am holding anything to do her any harm. "So, can I come in?"

Adria looks toward the sky. I don't know why 'cause it's cloudy. Then she looks at the baby and back at me again. I'm thinking she doesn't want to do this now, and I'm a few moments from asking all I need to know from her. "Sure, Lala, come on in. I've been meaning to call you, anyway," she finally decides.

That I don't doubt. Adria had always been the type of person who acted as though she could do no wrong, and things could be resolved at her convenience with a quick call.

We walk into her television room like we always have done when I visit. This time it is much more odd, especially after hearing the baby coo and exhale a few times while he's sleeping in her arms.

Adria plops down on the couch. I enjoy seeing her go through it. I like the fact she is out of her fake element and so exposed as being a fraud. Her place is much more out of whack than normal. It's evident she hasn't showered in days because she doesn't look fresh. Her hair is a mess. She needs tracks more than Puffy. Her hands are still fat, nails chipped and frayed, while her clothes are wrinkled and utterly shabby. She has on sweatpants that are way too tight and a football jersey so old the numbers are faded.

"So, how have you been?" Adria wants to know.

"I'm fine, all things considering," I say somewhat quickly.

"That's good." She looks at the baby in her arms, then at me. "Look, Lala, I never in a million years would plan what happened between us."

"You don't have an obligation to explain," I lie.

"Yeah right." She tries to chuckle. "This was wrong, Lala. The way things happened—I mean I really wanted to tell you."

I don't want to lose my temper but I have been grappling with the same thing since I found out. "Adria, I just want to know why. I want to know how could you keep this from me. Do you know how many opportunities you had to tell me about this?"

"Lala, I know, and I was going to tell you..."

I cut her off because I needed to know. "When? Why didn't you?"

Adria looks at the baby. "The day you talked me out of having that abortion, that's when I wanted to tell you. There were so many things running through my mind and when I decided to have the baby, at that moment, I wanted to tell you, but just couldn't bring myself around to do it."

"So, that entire night I stayed up with you to talk you out of killing that baby in your arms, the entire time, you knew it was Keith's?"

Adria nods her head yes and we sit still for about fifteen minutes without any words and only a few deep breaths from the baby.

I finally manage to say my piece. "So tell me about Keith, Adria. I just don't understand why you two ended up doing this; how even? My friend and my man make a child. I've cried so much my tear ducts wouldn't function if I begged them to."

Adria's face becomes molded. It is tight and wondrous.

"Adria, can you tell me?"

"Lala, I don't know. It just happened."

I feel a spike in my blood pressure. "No, you just don't let this type of thing happen, Adria." I lower my quivering voice. "Tell me now, Adria, what made you do this to me?"

"The thing with Keith. It wasn't even that deep, Lala. I mean it wasn't supposed to happen like this."

"What do you mean 'like this'?"

"I don't know, Lala. It just happened."

"'*Just happened*'?" I am trying to stay calm out of respect for the baby, so I whisper, "Would you stop fuckin' saying that it 'just happened.' Nothing *just happens*."

"I saw him at a club a few times. He was hanging out with a group of guys and we just started to chat."

"So, just from talking with my man, you end up fucking him, then having a baby."

"No, no, we would have really good conversations and most of them were about you."

"Me?"

"Keith had been upset with you, for a while."

"About what?"

"He told me that he was having issues with you."

"What kind of issues?"

"Something or another about not being able to complete the act of sex with you, when you two made love."

"Keith told you that?"

"Said he didn't feel like you two were really intimate because you guys were practicing the withdrawal method."

"So, you decide to fuck him because of that?"

"No, it wasn't even that serious."

"Looks that serious now."

"We just started to flirt at the club."

"So, you were sneaking around with him?"

"Not really."

"Well, what were you doing?"

"We just agreed unofficially to meet there and things began to get a bit out of hand."

"I'd say so…"

"We only did it once, Lala. I swear to you."

"One time?"

"That's it."

"Where?"

"At the Sheraton in Buckhead."

"No protection?"

"Keith decided that we knew each other long enough, and I didn't have any concerns about him because he had been with you so long."

"Gee, thanks."

Our conversation is interrupted when the baby begins to cry. Adria takes him off her shoulder to see what's wrong, and I, for the second time, see Keith all through him. My stomach is turning queasy and wanting my own child by Keith at the same time. Adria tells me it's feeding time. But the baby won't latch on to her nipples, and she is getting upset and has to call her lactationist to get instruction. We attempt a few times to continue our conversation over the baby's wailing after he eats, but I decide it's time to leave.

I can only drive halfway down the street before the pain of talking to Adria takes over. I have to stop and let it all out. I cry so hard that my stomach begins to ache, then my pain turns into complete anger. The episode lasts about thirty minutes. I collect myself and call Sydney. Forget Keith right now.

Sydney helps me to collect myself, then encourages me to meet him at the club. I wipe my tears away, reach for the rearview mirror to check my makeup and puffy eyes, and that's when I notice Keith's car turning into Adria's complex.

I pull up behind Keith's car in front of Adria's before he can get out of his car.

"Surprised to see me?"

"Not really. So, what're you doing out here?"

I look at Keith wondering if he thinks his answer is sufficient.

"Don't worry about me, Keith. The question is, what the hell are *you* doing here?"

Keith tries to laugh me off and turns around. He begins to walk toward Adria's doorstep as though he doesn't owe me shit.

"Where are you going?"

He is standing with his back toward me at Adria's door. "Well, now you know, Lala, I want to see my son."

Keith's tone is definite. It is strong. It is the first time I have heard any passion in his voice about his child, and I am not ashamed to tell him I can't handle it.

Finally, he turns around to face me. "Sorry, Lala, but you have to deal with it."

I start to cry on the spot. "'Deal with it'? I mean I understand you wanting to see him, but is that all you can say to me after I invested six years of my life for you?"

"For me?"

"Yes, you, Keith."

"Lala, get real. Those years were for you. You stayed with me so that you could say that you had a man."

"Ah, yeah. What's your point, asshole?"

"The point is…it's over. I thought about this whole thing and there's no way in hell I'm going to let my son grow up without a father in his life. Hell, even you should know me better than that. What we've been doin' has been a mistake. We need to move on."

That's when Adria opens the door and looks out. Keith tells her everything is okay.

"No, don't you believe that shit, Adria. Everything is not okay," I shout to her.

"Lala, what are you still doing here?"

"What the fuck you mean, still?" Keith asks.

Adria and Keith are up on the porch whispering so I move closer to the door and want to get the situation out in the open and discussed.

"Look, I don't know why you're creeping up here, Lala. If you think you're going to start some shit, like the day in the garage, in my car, you have another thing coming."

Adria shouts, "Lala, would you please leave?"

"Leave?"

"Yes, leave."

"Bitch, I ain't going anywhere! You fuckin,' man-stealing bitch."

"Look, if he was yours, I wouldn't have got him in the first place, now would I?"

"Look, we are too old to be out here like some high school kids discussing this," Keith decides.

"Well, let's discuss this inside then," I say to them. My tears are flowing and I don't care.

Keith looks at Adria, then me.

"There's nothing to discuss, Lala."

"What are you talking about?"

"This is where I want to be," he tells me.

"You want to be here?"

"That's right."

"With her?"

"And my son," Keith clarifies.

"I thought we were working through this, Keith?"

"He already told me, Lala," Adria says. "It was just break-up sex. That's all, break-up sex, and I understand—you guys have history—and you need to understand my child needs a father."

We are all quiet, looking at one another and what the situation has become, then Adria grabs Keith's arm to pull him inside.

Adria looks at me. "Lala, I'm sorry it has to be like this. I'm not raising a child alone." Before I say one word, she shuts the door and I am left standing alone.

Chapter 10

On my way to the club, Sydney calls to tell me to meet him in the parking lot. Evidently, there is a gathering inside and he doesn't think I would want to be around a bunch of partygoers. He is right. When I pull into the graveled one-way-in, one-way-out, squared-off-by-three-brick-buildings lot, I notice a man leaning down talking to Sydney through the window of his car. When they notice me, he walks away. Sydney waves me over and I pull next to his almond-colored 740 BMW, then roll down my window.

"C'mon, get in," he says to me.

I grab my things, open the passenger side, get inside and sink down as far as I can go into the leather seat of the car without saying a word. I can only focus my eyes on the dim-lit, orange-colored dashboard of the car because I am embarrassed. I do notice the car is cleaned immaculately inside and I can smell the fresh leather on the seats along with Sydney's cologne.

"Okay?"

"Not really," I tell him.

Sydney is looking out into the street at the passing cars. "Bad discussion, huh?"

"The worst. The truth hurts, Sydney."

"She told you more than you were expecting?"

"Not only that. I saw it with my own two eyes. I am so fuckin' mad at myself."

"Just know I'm here for you. You don't have to keep it all bottled up inside."

"You just don't do friends this way, Sydney. Adria tried to spin this thing like it was just a one-nighter turned bad. Those two had been having mental foreplay leading up to the sex."

Sydney chuckles. "My mother always would tell my sisters that friends were dangerous."

"I wish I wouldn't have been so stupid."

"You weren't. You were trusting. You trusted your man and your friend and there's nothing wrong with that."

"They slept together, then acted as though it was business as usual."

"Of course, if it weren't for the baby you would have never known."

Sydney struck a chord because I knew he was right. The baby had turned out to be the telling tale.

"It's just all so amazing. You know, Adria would have been the first person I would've run to if Keith and I ever had problems. She knew so much about our relationship. I told her too much and she took advantage of her knowledge of my relationship at my expense."

"Don't blame yourself. They both were wrong but now you just have to decide if it's really worth getting back with him or move on."

I lift myself up from the seat a bit. "Or decide to get revenge."

"Revenge? Never knew it was an option you were contemplating."

"It wasn't, not until I saw Keith on his way over to Adria's after I left. He told me he had business with a client and he ends up over her place—with his new family."

"Tell me you didn't follow him…"

"I didn't. He showed up when I'm in the car crying after I leave her place, then we all have words. I feel like a fool, Sydney. I feel like what they've done to me deserves some type of punishment."

Sydney lights a cigar. "Some get back, huh?"

"Absolutely." I turn my body around and look at Sydney. "Didn't you tell me you solved problems?"

Sydney blows out a perfect smoke ring and looks at me. "I do. There's no denying that."

Chapter 11

I'm pissed now. Sydney suggests we go for a drive and I agree. He calls the compartment in between our seats his mini bar and offers me my choice of cute little liquor bottles like the ones Halle Berry's character drank in the movie *Monsters Ball* just before she told the white man to make her *feel good*. Sydney has it all. There is a small bag of ice, a bottle of ginger ale for mixing, and a sexy, clear, plastic cup to drink out of. I choose Canadian Mist mixed with the ale and twirl the ice with my finger as Sydney drives. Sydney chooses Jose Cuervo.

The lights of downtown Atlanta and the jazz softly blaring from the speakers are good for us. Relaxing but definitely reflecting.

"Ever since I moved here, I've never wanted to leave," explains Sydney. "Much better than Mississippi, I tell you that, much better."

"Do this often, Sydney?"

"You mean, get away, take a drive and relax?"

"Yes."

"Not as much as I used to—with the gas prices being

so high and all. But I do every now and then. You'll be amazed by how much it takes the edge off."

I feel Sydney look at me, then back at the road.

"So you finished now. Finished with Keith?"

"Like you'll never believe. He could die and eat shit, for all I care. There should be some type of law against what he's done."

"No laws. But there's always retribution, sweetheart. It's just a matter of how much you really want the person who's wronged you to pay."

I spurt out without any real intention, "How 'bout his life. Give me his fuckin' life."

Sydney pulls out his lighter and I'm amazed how he lights and drives with the smoke billowing in his eyes all at the same time. The sound of his lighter closing metal to metal gets my attention even more.

"Now that can be arranged," Sydney admits without looking over at me.

Chapter 12

I always knew Sydney was a dangerous man. It was painted on him by the way he dressed and presented himself. We hit every major street downtown. By the time he drops me off, I am aware of just how hazardous this man can really be.

He finally broke it down and told me exactly how he solved problems. He had friends who would do anything for him. A ruthless bunch of motherfuckers whose middle names were pain and more pain. I would be scared to look any of these guys in the eyes. Sydney told me way more than I ever wanted to know about these men. I know what he tells me, I will take to my grave and never repeat. Just the thought of some fools being after me was enough to throw what I was told in the *I don't know shit* memory bank. I did become interested in the reasons people would come to him. Sydney revealed to me that they all felt slighted and degraded in some form or fashion. Most of the time they wanted relief from their situations. Ordinary people, too, as well as the well off. I have to admit some of the things Sydney was involved in were way over my head.

But after seeing Keith and Adria standing on her porch in their unified front, I wanted payback on Keith's ass. Up until that point, chasing Keith in his car and hearing him scream like a little girl was good enough for me. But right then, it wasn't. The chase only made him lose his breath. I had scars and maybe was scarred for life. I'd put my trust in this man to take care of me and start a family, so one day I, too, could hold my child in my arms like Adria. But it was all a memory now. So I decided that payback for Keith was in order. He needed to get his and I told Sydney so.

Sydney is so calm concerning my wishes. It's like another day at the office for him. I notice he doesn't look at me any differently concerning my decision. He understands pain and I have a feeling he is going to be a part of Keith's payback because of the bond we have created. I end up giving Sydney all the information about Keith and Adria that I know. He needs to do his own investigation to see how Keith moves around, and in the meantime, decide how to deal with him. Sydney thought it best if we stopped meeting as well as talking on the phone. I don't even question his reasoning.

Chapter 13

After three weeks of waiting to hear from Sydney, I begin to wonder if he is still going to go through with my request. The only reason I know he hasn't at this point is because I called Keith's office a few times and hung up when he answered the phone. To make matters worse, Adria showed up at the office with the baby, of course, just three days after I decided to go back to work.

All of a sudden things start to happen.

After work I find a note taped to the steering wheel of my car. It's kind of unsettling at first, because I always lock my car doors, and there is no trace that my car has been tampered with. The note reads:

AFTER TONIGHT NO MORE PAIN.

There are also instructions for me to burn the note,

call a pager from a phone booth, and place the numbers "404" to acknowledge the plan was still a go.

I drive to a gas station, call the pager, and drive off, realizing Keith is about to finally get his.

At this point, I can't even go home after realizing what is about to happen. I stay in my car and, of all the things to do, I drive around Interstate 285 at least two-and-a-half times trying to buy time and thinking about the unknown.

Around seven o'clock, I decide to get something to eat and go into an Applebee's. I find a seat right next to a window looking out into the streets. I order a strawberry daiquiri and lemon-peppered wings. While I pick at my wings, I am drawn into listening to a conversation with a group of well-dressed, obviously smart and headstrong girls who had come into the restaurant minutes after me. They are on the topic of men and how trifling they are. One thing's for certain: they are absolutely pissed over a situation that apparently had one of their girls bawling uncontrollably. I am instantly drawn into their chat and could absolutely relate to the one being cheated on. I appreciate the fact that her girlfriends are there for her, so I turn around and let them know right before I order myself another drink. About thirty minutes later the girls are still going at it. That's when I realize that the game has no boundaries, and there is truly no reason I should have Keith hurt. For some reason, as I listen to the girls complain about the doggish things men do, I come to the conclusion that we cannot make them love us and give us what we've always dreamed of if they truly don't want to. I realize while I sit and listen to the girls call men names and spew out deserving insults that it all doesn't matter because men have always been doggish and uncaring. Things will never change.

When I truly and fully understand, I realize my request to Sydney is out of my character and not even worth the trouble. What if things get out of hand and somehow everything is traced back to me, and I spend the rest of my life in prison for a fool who didn't give a damn about me? I have a change of mind and decide that the best revenge will be to let Adria have Keith's sorry ass. No doubt that he will do the same thing to her.

Then it will be her turn to feel the same pain and in the long run, Keith will end up a miserable old man.

I take my cell phone out of my bag and call Sydney. For the first time since I've known him, he doesn't answer. About ten minutes later, he calls.

I answer, "Sydney, forget about it."

"Second thoughts?"

"It's just not worth it…" I want to explain but he cuts me off.

"Well, I gotta make a call. It might already be done."

"Really?"

"Call you back when I can."

I have another drink and all the while thinking that it's too late. Whatever happened is already done. I'm already remorseful. I'm in the process of pulling out the parking lot when my phone rings.

"Done," Sydney says.

I inhale. "Done?"

"Yes, I called them when they were en route and called it off."

I exhale. "Good. I thought it over. No need for that. They'll both get theirs. I put my word on it."

"The way they treated you, Lala, I'm sure they will. I am sure they will."

Chapter 14

Six months later.

I volunteer to be a youth counselor with the Mentoring Our Youth Association. I'm determined to teach a young boy how to be a man of his word and treat women with respect. On the first day, I am standing in the parking lot looking at the grass; enough for a pick-up game of football and a oil painting of kids smiling and holding hands on the side of the building.

When I walk inside, I can hear the bigger kids in the gym playing basketball. Down the hall, there are girls listening to music and dancing to the sounds of Ciara. The smaller kids have their own agenda and run back and forth through the center hallways.

"May I help you?"

The male voice comes from behind me so I have to turn around. I introduce myself and he tells me his name is Lorenzo Murray, the director of the center. The first thing that he does is excuse himself for the sweat dripping down his face from playing basketball in the gym. I am surprised to see that he was playing ball in dress pants and a blue button-down, but he mentions that some of the boys had baited him into a game of basketball. He looks to be about six feet two and in pretty good shape. His face is brown, covered with a light beard, and his eyes are light gray. He extends his hand and tells me he has been expecting me. I follow him to his office down the hall and past a desk where a lady sits answering the phones and attending to any problem the kids may have. When I sit down across from his desk, I notice a diploma from Eastern Michigan University with 1992 as his graduation date.

"So, welcome home," he says proudly.

"Excuse me?"

"Welcome home. That's what the kids call this place."

"Really?"

"Absolutely. We give them everything a home should have: discipline, encouragement, hot meals, and plenty of love."

"Sounds like home to me."

He smiles. "We try very hard here, Ms. Stewart."

"Please, Lala Paige."

"Okay, Lala. First off, let me tell you that we are very happy to have you."

"Why thank you."

"And I mean that. You know a lot of people think this place runs on its own. But we have some really dedicated people who work here. We have a full-time staff of ten here at the center but we depend heavily on our counselors. You will be able to reach these kids and help them obtain the necessary skills in life."

"Well, I'm ready to do my part."

"We have so many kids here. They are all ages. I have to be quite honest with you. Some of our older kids, as you may imagine, they already know it all."

He looks around and lowers his voice. "You really can't tell them shit because they already know what you want to tell them." He laughs.

"Been there too..."

"Haven't we all? And most of us are afraid to admit it. I usually try to take all the kids over fifteen and work with them in different types of groups. Right now we have a dire need for help with the younger crowd, the six-to-nine age group."

I smile.

"These are the children who really need help. Most of them are born with no fathers. Let me correct that... no fathers who care."

"Oh, I understand. I understand completely."

Chapter 15

I sit and chat with Lorenzo close to an hour. There is no mistake that Lorenzo loves his job. He has observed parents dealing with their kids. His main concern is based on the children and their parents, who instead of parenting, still chase their own childhood dreams at the expense of the kids.

Our conversation is long enough to let him know that I am eager to get started. I fill out some paperwork, then follow him into the part of the center where the young kids hang out. We bypass the gym. The kids inside seem to be fifteen years old or older but it's always so hard to tell. Then we walk past a classroom full of nine-year-old girls who are working on a vibrant dance routine. We then venture down the hall and into a room full of bright-eyed younger kids—some watching television, some playing board games, others chasing each other and screaming their beautiful heads off.

"Well, here we are." Lorenzo is all smiles.

"They're all so cute!"

"These are my pride and joy. Young, impressionable

minds—the innocent and sweet who, with our help, have the best chance to succeed." Lorenzo swoops up one of the young ones who is in full stride. At my first glance, I can't tell the sex of the child.

"Boy, didn't I ask you to tell your mama to get your hair cut?" By this time, the cheerful tyke is high in the air in Lorenzo's outstretched arms.

"Put me down," the boy screams. There is no doubt he is having the time of his life suspended in air.

"I tell you what. I'll let you down if you get a haircut."

The boy has a big smile. "I'm getting braids like Snoop!"

"You're getting braids?"

"Yes, they goin' to go this way and this way."

"Why are you getting braids, man?"

"'Cause I like 'em. They cool!"

Lorenzo looks up at him. "Aight, just make sure they nice and neat, okay?"

"Okay," the little one says.

Lorenzo puts him down, then tells the boy to shake on it. When he does, Lorenzo makes him shake again. This time Lorenzo tells him to apply more pressure for a firm handshake. After the boy does, he is off and running again—chasing his next victim.

Chapter 16

I walk around the room and it feels good to talk with the children. Their energy level is definitely unexpected and something I know I'm going to have to get used to. They ask tons of questions. Some of them want to know my name, others if I am Lorenzo's girlfriend. I am even asked if I am in—of all people—Jay-Z's video. When I look around I think I've had said hello to everyone. But there is one little chocolate boy who is really into the two palm-sized rubber balls that he is playing with. I bend over and ask him, "Can I see those?"

He picks up the balls and squeezes them, not knowing if he should put them behind his back. He looks at me with the brightest eyes ever.

"Goin' to give 'em back?"

I smile, almost laugh. "Yes…"

"That's what er'body say."

"They do?"

"Yes, then they take off and run with them 'cause they know I can't catch 'em."

"Well, I won't run," I let him know.

"Promise?"

"I promise."

I sit down on the floor with the little boy, and we roll the balls back and forth for at least a half-hour.

"So, what's your name?"

"My name is Sean and I'm six."

"Sean, what a nice name and you're a big boy, too!"

"Thank you."

"I'm Lala."

"You wanna see my money?"

"You have money?"

"Yes."

"How much do you have?"

"I have enough to buy a soda," Sean says. Then he pulls some change out of his pocket and shows it to me. "See…"

"Let me see what you have there…" I look into his hand and there are two dimes and a nickel. I know he doesn't have enough for a soda and decide that I will buy.

"You want me to buy you one, too," Sean says with confidence.

"Sure, I'll take one. Lead the way."

Chapter 17

I can't get enough of Sean after the first day and our bond is getting stronger after four weeks. This little boy has won my heart a hundred times over. At this point Lorenzo confided that he is pleased that I chose Sean to mentor. I found out that Sean had been coming into the center for about three months. He walked in the door with three of his sisters who were all much older, but after a week or two, the girls never returned.

By organization rules, counselors are only allowed to meet with the kids at the center for the first month. Afterward, they are required to meet the parents. It was time for me to do exactly that.

Sean doesn't live far from the center. I park my car there and decide to walk through the neighborhood to his house. It is such a pretty day and the scent of autumn is in the air. I have taken off work early to meet Sean after school. It was a good thing that I did because for some reason, Adria was looking in my direction more than usual, like she had something to say.

The walk seems to do me some good because it is allowing me to forget about Adria's stares and think about Sean and all the positive things that will come out of being his mentor. When I arrive at his house, I stand right outside of the waist-high fence leading up to his porch to get my bearings. I'm a little nervous because it's my first meeting with Sean's parents and I don't know much about them. Sean's file at the center showed that his mother's name is Dorothy and his father's, Mark. She is a stay-at home mom and his father works as a consultant in the car-manufacturing industry. I asked Lorenzo if it was odd for kids with both parents at home to be involved in the center's activities but he didn't think so. He told me that, more than likely, they wanted the kids to meet other kids. Or they used their time away from home to get some much needed time together. I thoroughly understood.

Before I unlatch the fence to walk up to the door, I stare at the two-story, cream-colored house and quickly go over in my mind everything I want to talk about with Sean's parents.

Then I hear Sean's little voice ringing from an upstairs window. "Don't be scared, Lala. I don't have a dog."

I look up toward the window. I can barely see Sean's little dark-skinned face through the screen. "Boy...you scared me half to death," I tell him.

He yells down, "Well, I just wanted you to know, 'cause everybody that comes over my house think I gotta dog."

"They do?"

"Yes…"

"And why is that, Sean?"

"Because I used to, his name is Joey."

I am just about ready to open the gate, but Sean needs to clarify what he is saying to me before I touch the gate again. His tone for some reason is not definite. I look around the yard, then back up at Sean.

"So, you used to have a dog?"

"Um…hmm…"

"And his name *was*, Joey?"

"No, Lala. His name *is* Joey…"

"What do you mean *is*, Sean?"

"'Cause, that's his name."

"But if he's gone, what you mean to say is *was*."

"Lala, he's not gone anywhere."

"No?"

Sean says from the window with his lips as close to the screen as possible, "Uh…huh…"

"Well, where is he then?"

"I dunno…"

I step away from the gate a few steps and look around some more. "Boy, what do you mean, you don't know?"

I see his white teeth now, smiling through the screen. "I don't know where he is," he tells me in his squeaky, little voice.

"Wait a minute. You have a dog and you don't know where he is?"

"Yup."

"Okay…so, what kind of dog is it? A little one or big one, Sean?"

"He's a Rottweiler."

I pause a few seconds to get my doggy dictionary in my mind together. "You mean one of those big dogs with the big heads?"

"Yup…the same kind everybody's scared of—but not me. Lala, do you know his head is bigger than both of ours, smashed together?"

I'm nervous now and getting anxious for answers. "Well, Sean, tell me something right now, young man. When's the last time you saw him, Sweetie?"

"Yesterday, after dinner."

"Yesterday?"

"Umm…hmm," he sings.

"And where was he?"

"On the side of the fence you're on."

I snatch the gate open, step inside the yard, and close the gate behind me with the quickness. "Boy, if you don't come down here right this minute and open this door, I'll spank you. Now hurry up," I tell him.

Sean opens the door and has a huge smile on his face. When I see his little black face, I can't even be mad at him anymore for letting me stand outside with the possibilities of a killer dog being on the loose.

I give him a hug. "Hey, boy."

"Hey, Lala. Were you scared out there?"

"Yes…"

"I don't blame you." He snickers. "Joey's a real mean dude when he's hungry."

"Sean, where are your parents, boy?"

A deep voice startles me as his father makes his appearance from one of the rooms in the house. "Hi, I'm Mark," he says.

I extend my hand out to him. "Hello, I'm Lala and…"

"Lala, say no more, I've heard all about you."

I smile. "Well, I wonder who could have told you…"

Sean smiles and Mark places his hand on top of his son's head. "All I can say is, he's fallen head over heels with you."

"Well, I'm glad because I've fallen for him, too."

Mark offers me a glass of Kool-Aid and, when I accept, Sean grabs my hand and leads the way.

Chapter 18

My visit with Sean and his father is nice. We sit and talk close to an hour and I get a chance to chat with his sisters as Sean lays down the law to them—that I am his mentor and they will have to get their own. I am feeling good about my decision to mentor Sean as it seems like he comes from a good family. But I do find it kind of strange that his mother is not there to say hello.

I get a call from Sydney when I get home. His call is kind of a surprise because I am used to hearing from him closer to bedtime when he wants to know if I'm okay. He asks me out for a drink. Of course he is hanging out at his favorite spot. Since it has been quite a while since we actually saw each other, I decide to go see him.

I walk in around eight o'clock. I notice Sydney and feel awkward as I make my way over because I know his so called "friends" who do "things" for him are more than likely here, too.

Sydney notices my nervousness; before I sit down he stands up and gives me a reassuring hug. He always smells so good. His hug makes me feel better.

"C'mon, sit down," he says. "Everything's fine. You doin' okay?"

I smile up at him. Then, like a magician, he slides behind me and helps with my coat and my chair.

After my first Sea Breeze I decide to have another while Sydney works on his third cognac. We are having a really good visit, talking with Sydney face to face is much better than on the phone.

Sydney is looking down into his glass while he swirls his drink. "I have something to talk to you about."

"Dang… you sound all serious."

"I am."

He pauses.

"You're all right, aren't you?"

"Oh, yeah yeah."

"Well, what is it then? Got me all tensed up and shit."

Sydney looks from his glass.

"It's my wife."

"Your wife?"

"Nancy, she's interested in you," he says.

I knew Sydney was a different kind of man. But when he tells me that his wife is interested in me, a million thoughts run through my mind.

I sit up closer to the table and I know my eyes are squinted. "Interested in what?"

"Look, I don't know."

"Sydney, I have to tell you right now. I don't get down like that."

He grabs my hand. "Lala, look at me."

I give Sydney the "okay, talk to me" look.

"Do you think I would approach you like that?"

I giggle a bit. "Well, tell me something. I thought maybe you were trying to convince me to do some freaky shit. I mean, it's been a long time. But not that damn long. I tell you that right now."

"Look, I'd never put you out like that; this is me— Sydney."

"Well, what then?"

"I think she wants to talk to you."

I am quick. "About what, Sydney?"

"She didn't say."

"Wait a minute. How does she even know about me?"

Sydney is blunt before he sips the last bit of his cognac. He doesn't even struggle with the burn that he has to be struggling with after a gigantic gulp. Then he lifts his finger up for another. "I told her," he says, satisfied with his drink.

"You told her?"

"Yes, I told her. I heard her talking to her sister Sheila, who lives down in Macon and of course, Sheila's been fucked up with me and wanting space from her sister— so I overhear her filling Nancy's head up with utter bullshit."

I even felt the confused look on my face.

"Remember I told you about our agreement?"

"The open thing, right?"

"Yes, our relationship. We agreed to tell one another anything the other wanted to know about the specific person we had been spending time with."

"So, I guess she asked you about me?"

"Sure did."

"And? What'd she say, Sydney? What did you tell her? Give me something."

"I explained to her that you were a very lovely, young lady and I enjoyed your company."

"That's it?"

"That is it," he makes certain.

"And for that, she wants to talk to me?"

"Evidently," he guarantees.

"Really?"

Sydney nods his head.

"This is all too confusing. I mean…"

"So, you'll do it?"

I look at my watch and it's past the time I told Sydney that I would stay. I pull out my credit card and place it on the bill. "Look, Sydney, I would have to really think about it. You sure she really wants to meet me?" Sydney smiles with his eyes and barely nods his head back and forth.

Sydney picks up my card and holds it out for me. "Let me ask you a question."

"Okay?"

"Have you ever paid for anything while you've dined with me?"

Pause. "Well, no…"

"Okay then, and you're not going to start now. Here, take this. You shouldn't be working with these things, anyway. Credit cards are passé," he informs.

"Oh really." I smile back at Sydney.

"Their only intention is to hold a sista down."

I grab my card. "Oh, really now?"

"Absolutely, matter of fact, if you're having credit problems, I have a guy who can wipe it all clean in a punch of a button as sure as my name is…"

I have to cut him off. "I'm sure you do, Sydney," I tell him, laughing. "But no thanks…"

Chapter 19

I spend most of the next day with Sean at the zoo. We are there until we see every animal and take our turn on every ride. Sean is enjoying the attention and I am happy that he is. On the way home, Sean is telling me what he wants to be when he is all grown up. He goes from a fireman, to policeman, and then a racecar driver. All of a sudden he stops talking while we are sitting at a stoplight.

I turn to him and follow his eyes out the passenger's side window. At my first glance, I see a man looking down into a trash container on the corner searching for food, and a woman sitting under a bus shelter on a bench in the corner next to the Plexiglas. Her head is wrapped with a black do-rag and she is wearing a gray dress, brimmed hat made for a man, and soft-heel shoes. Her clothes are dingy and frayed, but interestingly, her face is made up perfectly which really draws my attention to her. As she reaches into her purse, she pulls out a small bottle that looks like whiskey, then takes a hard swig from it.

I drive a few blocks and pull over to the curb, when I realize Sean is crying. He tells me that the lady sitting on the bench is his mother, and he has not seen her, in his words, "in a long, long time."

Chapter 20

Lorenzo didn't prep me for this. I can't get Sean to stop crying. Nothing I say is soothing him, and I'm confused about what he is uttering to me over his cries about his mother. I'm under the impression that his mother lives at home with him. After a while it's apparent that he's sure it was his mother at the bus stop. He is all-out hysterical. I don't know what to do or say to him. At the same time, I feel so sorry for him because he is hurting.

I am undecided when Sean asks me to turn around so that he can see his mother again. Since she is at a bus stop, I don't have a long time to make up my mind. Eventually, Sean's cries overcome any thought process that I am going through. I do a U-turn and travel the few blocks back to where we saw his mother sitting. I pull up close to the bus stop next to the curb. We look up toward the bench, but she is gone. The homeless man looking in the trashcan is still there sifting through a Burger King wrapper and wiping down what is left from a hamburger. I step out my car and ask him did he see where the lady sitting on the bench went. He tells me he didn't, then asks me for a dollar. I give him two and that's when he tells me the lady we are looking for is named Dorothy.

It is ultra quiet in the car all the way back to Sean's house. I want him to relax but he hasn't. Matter of fact, he is worse off because he wants to know how the homeless man knew his mother's name. When I finally get Sean home, there is no hiding that he's in a funk. His eyes are swollen from crying; he has tear stains running down his cheeks When he tells me good-bye, his voice is barely audible and crackly to where it almost makes me cry.

Mark is outside raking leaves when we pull into the driveway. When he sees Sean run into the house, he raises his gloved hands toward the sky, then looks at me as I make my way over to him. Sean runs so fast and hard that you hear, through the screen door of the house, his little feet hitting the hardwood flooring on the steps. He doesn't think twice about stopping when his father calls out for him. That's when Mark looks at me more closely. His eyes are wondering. He bends over and picks up his rake and moves a small pile of golden leaves closer to a pile next to a paper bag. "He didn't want to leave the zoo, did he?"

"No, that's not it. He had a wonderful time," I assure him.

"Well, what's wrong with him then?"

"Sean seems to think he saw his mother today," I comment. The moment, for some reason, consciously makes me feel as though I am stepping into rippling water for the first time.

Mark looks up from the leaves quickly at the mention of Sean's mother. I don't know how to take his reaction.

"What do you mean, he saw his mother?" His voice is edgy now. Nothing like I had ever heard from him.

I take my time to answer him. I want to be clear. "Well, we were on our way back here and while I was stopped at a red light, he began to cry. When I asked him why, he said that he saw his mother sitting on a bench at a bus stop."

Mark quickly dismisses my information. "That boy," he says, trying to remove doubt. "He's so sensitive. She's probably on her way here this very moment," he explains.

"Here?"

"Yeah, home from work. She's been back a few days now. Her car…"

I realize Mark is going to lie to me, so I cut him off, "Sean already mentioned that he hasn't seen her."

"Say what?"

"He told me she hasn't been here in a long time, Mark."

Mark takes a deep breath and has what seems like a drama-filled glance into the past with his thoughts. I am patient and don't force the issue because he is a terrible liar so far. I think that just being quiet and staring him down will let me in on what is going on that much quicker.

His second deep sigh of anxiety comes right before he starts to speak again.

"Okay, here's the deal. She doesn't live here anymore. She's been gone almost four months."

"Four months?" It's all I can say. But at least it is in line with what Sean had told me.

Mark starts to rake again. I take his getting back to work as a polite way of telling me that he is finished with the topic. But I can't let it go there. Sean is wiped out at the sight of seeing his mother. I want to understand a little better what is going on. I remember during my first visit, that Mark spoke as if she were in the house but just not at home.

He looks at me. "You're confused, right?"

I nod yes.

Mark details, "She left. I don't know how else to put it. She left us all and to tell you the truth, it's been hell to deal with."

"I can imagine. But Sean never mentioned it before and he seemed so happy about things in his life."

"What can I say? I'm bringing him up like a soldier. He is adapting from the shock of his mother leaving. One night she tucks him in the bed good night and when he wakes up, I'm reading a note saying that she's leaving but she 'loves them all'...I mean...fuck me."

"Did she give a reason?"

"Not one damn word. What kind of woman leaves her kids?"

"Mark, I don't know. But when I went back to where she was so Sean could talk to her, she was gone."

"Look, I appreciate your concern. But I don't want Sean having any contact with her, you got that?"

"Sure…sure, Mark, anything you say."

Chapter 21

I am taken aback a bit by Mark's attitude, so I leave wondering why he doesn't want Sean to see his mom. Maybe he is still upset with his wife leaving him; I could definitely relate to that, so I digress and try to relax my mind.

I know that Lorenzo is at the center, and I call him to let him know that I am on my way. He says he's dying for a real meal and invites me to meet him at Gladys Knight's downtown for a bite to eat. He is already there when I arrive. He waves me over to the table. I work my way around the hostess who is already placing the table with collards, fried chicken, candied yams, corn bread, and the sweet tea has already been poured.

"So, what are you going to do now?" Lorenzo wants to know after I fill him in on what is going on with Sean. "Are you going to let what happened be and walk out of his life, or will you continue with the program?"

"Oh, I'm no quitter, but what's your opinion on the situation?"

"Look, there are over twenty-five thousand boys alone

registered with the boys club and our center in Atlanta alone. All of them, looking for love and direction."

Lorenzo takes a sip of his tea. "Sometimes I wonder why people even go through the trouble of making kids when they don't want to take care of them."

"So what should I do?"

"Continue to spend time with Sean and give him all that you can. Hopefully, his father doesn't pull him from the center."

"Oh, I hope not. That little boy needs me more than ever now."

"Well, I've seen it done so don't overstep—walk lightly."

"But my question is…where are the lines? The boy wants his mother."

"It's never easy, never black and white. Every kid nowadays has their own problems that need specialized attention. I mean, some complex shit—hell, we all do."

"Well, I want to help Sean, more than ever now."

"I understand and you will," Lorenzo consoles.

We reflect on our conversation, then move on.

"You know, I actually joined the center with the expectation of reaching a young man to teach him how to treat a woman."

Lorenzo kind of smiles. "Is-that-right…"

I smile right back at him. "Yeah, you know. Have respect, learn how to communicate, and have patience. And look, now, the boy I choose to work with—his mother is responsible for being the one who destroys a family."

"You can still instill it in him, though. All is not lost."

"How's that?"

"By teaching him, relationships are a people thing, something everyone needs to work at so they won't end up hurting those that love them." There is a pause 'cause Lorenzo takes a sip of tea. "So, what terrible situation put you in that frame of mind in the first place?"

"Oh, spare me. You-do-not-want to know…"

"Trust me, I do."

Chapter 22

I sit with Lorenzo for the next hour telling him about all the drama I had gone through with Keith and Adria. I tell him about the baby, about our plans to marry, how my girlfriend steals my man, and how they are now living together. It's almost funny now because time reveals that it was all bullshit. The only thing I was so very much upset about was all the time I wasted with Keith. Thinking about it almost brings tears to my eyes because I know I am never going to get all those years back. So many good years of my life down the drain.

Lorenzo doesn't make me feel any better when he lets me know that he didn't even realize women let men string them along in such a fashion. Then I understand what he means when he begins to tell me how his last breakup was because he waited too long to make some type of commitment. I immediately kick myself knowing that there are women out there who don't play that shit when it comes to their lives. I can tell his last relationship was deep because he speaks so passionately about it, even though he tries his best to make it as though he couldn't care less.

When I get home, I sit down and try to remember how I truly felt when my parents split up. I couldn't put myself directly in Sean's position because when they decided they couldn't take being together anymore, I was in high school and really didn't want to be bothered with either of them, anyway. But I realized it was so different for Sean. I knew that he had his sisters to latch on to, but like his father told me when we first met, he was no longer their baby brother; to them he was a pest who did nothing but get in the way now.

Looking back, there was no way that I could have handled that my mother was no longer around at such a young age. I wanted that boy to feel whole and see his mother. I understood completely that his father didn't want me to take Sean to see his mother but not the reason why. As I thought about what was at stake, I decided that maybe I should go and talk to her myself. Do nothing more than tell her that Sean loves and misses her very much. I thought she would appreciate that; what mother wouldn't?

Chapter 23

So, I try nonstop for weeks to find Dorothy without anyone's knowledge. I don't want to get Sean's hopes up high and definitely didn't want to piss off his father. By this time the poor, little boy is hurting and becoming more withdrawn by the minute.

One Sunday morning, I can't take it any longer. After spending most of Saturday night sitting in my car cruising the streets looking for Dorothy, I awake with nothing more on my mind than to get back on the streets to find her. I get in my car, grab a cup of coffee from Quick Trip, and venture back downtown to the exact spot where we saw her.

When I pull up to the Plexiglas-covered bus stop, it is empty. I sit in my car directly in front for about twenty minutes peering out on the block. I look for Dorothy until a bus on its route pulls up behind me and blasts its horn a few times for me to move out the way. I drive around the corner and park my car at a meter, then walk back to the stop. I come to the conclusion that since the homeless man knew her name, more than likely she had been living close by and had developed a reputation.

There is a coffee shop on the corner. I go inside and order another cup of coffee that I don't even touch, then sit by the window. After a few minutes, I begin to notice more people on the street, particularly homeless, who are walking by and seemingly getting ready for their day wandering the street. I leave the shop and walk toward the direction the homeless people are coming from. After about two blocks east of the bus stop, I notice a church. People are filing out a side door. I stand still for a moment to see what is going on and realize it's a shelter for the homeless. The church is white with a perfectly manicured yard with a huge tree that towers over the structure.

I approach a man and stand in front of him to get his attention. "Excuse me…"

He looks at me oddly at first, then he smiles. He isn't trying to hide the fact that he has only one front tooth. He is wearing a pair of faded blue jeans, a red T-shirt, and old-school Converse All-Star tennis shoes that are at least two sizes too big for him. A blue jean hat sits crumpled on his head,

He takes off his hat, pushes it into his chest, then nods. "Yes, ma'am…"

"Can you tell me about this place?" I point to the shelter.

He turns around and looks at the shelter, then back at me. "Oh, yes, indeed. Sure can. It's where I sleep and eat." He pulls at his jeans to keep them around his waist.

"Is it open?"

"Uh, yes, ma'am, it is. But right now, it's eleven o'clock. Unless you gonna work up in there and get lunch ready or clean, you have to leave until eight o'clock tonight."

"Are there any women staying there?"

"Oh, sure it is. Women, children, entire families. Times are hard and the shelter don't turn too many people away unless, of course, you're up to no good."

I take another glance at the shelter. "So, do you know a lady named Dorothy?"

He is quick to respond. "Oh, hell yeah, I know her."

"Really?"

"That's right. She's a pretty little thing. Dorothy don't play, either. Just the other day I walked up to her just to let her know I thought she was looking mighty fine, and you would have thought I put my hands on her ass or something. Oh yeah, Dorothy is up inside there, you hear me..." He smashes on his hat and walks away, still mumbling about his encounter with Dorothy.

I wait another five minutes with a close eye on the side door before I decide to go inside and talk to Dorothy. I am hesitant because the idea to come and look for her seemed like a good idea at first. But as I look around at the people coming out of the shelter, it dawns on me that what she is going through has to really be deep in order for her to leave her kids and comfortable home to be holed up in a shelter. Plus, I am kind of scared because I have never been in a shelter, but I push on for Sean.

Chapter 24

I finally get the courage to walk through the shelter door Immediately I can feel the eyes of the people who are standing, leering in the hallway on me. I quickly figure out that we are all in a basement. The basement has very old tile on the floors and the walls are made of cinderblocks and painted yellow. Some of the people inside are making sure they have all of their belongings before they venture out for another day in the streets. Others seem to be standing in a line waiting for something.

Then there is a shoutout to them.

"Okay! Who wants to work in the kitchen for lunch?" I easily recognize the voice as being tired and female. Her voice reminds me of my grandmother, who used to scream out for me to come inside to eat. The woman's voice is very strong. "I'm going to pick somebody who ain't worked back there before because I'm tired of ya'll, tryin' to snack on the food when you should be getting it ready for lunch."

"Ahh, c'mon, bitch," a dark-skinned man sings out. He

is skinny and about six feet eight but it doesn't seem like anyone in the hallway is scared of him. "It's the same thing with you every day," he whines. "Just pick some peoples so we can get out this crowded-ass hallway."

"Well, Leon," she shoots back. "I know it's not going to be your sorry, frail, fuckin' ass today!" There are a few laughs from people in the hallway. The lady yelling out directions is too far away for me to see what she looks like.

Leon shoots back, "Aww, fuck you, bitch."

"See now, your skinny ass will be scrubbing toilets, okay... I was goin' to put you on the hot biscuit tray but now, everybody, Leon, will be scrubbing toilets today," she brags. "Make sure you don't touch him 'cause we fresh outta plastic gloves. Now, how you like that, motherfucka!"

Leon runs out the side door and we hear the door slam shut. "Fuck that," he yells back.

It doesn't take long for the lady screaming directions to name those who would be working in the kitchen, then she chooses even faster jobs that need to be done. The people standing in the hallway quickly disperse, and I find myself being the only one still standing. A lady with a clipboard in her hand turns the corner into the hallway. I take her to be the voice I had been listening to.

She looks me up and down before she speaks. "May I help you?"

I smile at her. "Yes, I'm here looking for someone."

She gives me another once-over. "You don't look like an undercover detective. But who knows? I've heard about all the scandalous shit the police department gets into nowadays. Dressin' girls up like prostitutes and propositioning men. Hell, I tell you right now, if I was a man and one of those bunched-up titty women approached me, I would probably want to do them, too."

"No, no…" She won't let me get a word in.

"But I can tell you right now, officer. I screen everybody that walks through these doors, and as far as I can tell, everybody's clean." Then she extends her hand to me. "By the way, my name is Rosita. I run this place."

"Hi, Rosita, my name is Lala. It's good to know you keep an eye out for people here, but I'm not with the police."

"No?"

"No, I'm not."

"Why didn't you say that in the first place?"

"Believe me, I tried."

"Well, what can I do for you?"

"I'm looking for a lady."

"Lady got a name?"

"Yes, her name is Dorothy."

There is a pause from Rosita. That's when I get a good chance to look at her bronze face, which has small moles painted on, but not enough of them to be annoying. She is a big woman, with big eyes that make you feel comfortable talking to her. Rosita is big enough to fight a man if she has to. About five feet ten and a whole lot of pounds. I wouldn't even put it past her if she had fought a few. Her hands are big and she is wearing a man's button-down shirt that is open over a T-shirt and jeans. She looks down at her clipboard before she answers me. "Good or bad?" she inquires.

"Excuse me?"

"Good or bad news?" she repeats. "People got so much on their minds around here I just like to know when something good is happening in their lives. You know, it kinda brings me joy, too."

"It's about her son," I answer.

"Son?"

"Yes, her seven-year-old named Sean."

"She ain't never mentioned to me about no son. But then again, she don't even talk too much," Rosita explains.

"I'm his counselor at the youth center and he's just worried about her and I want her to know that."

"Well, I guess that's good news," Rosita says. "I mean, having someone thinking about you is good news, wouldn't you say?"

"Absolutely," I agree. "Absolutely…"

Chapter 25

I follow Rosita through the shelter to where she thinks Dorothy is located. On the way, Rosita only has good words about Dorothy except that she is very quiet. She would leave the shelter once or twice a day When she returned she would be even more withdrawn from being social with anyone who tried to talk to her. She said that Dorothy was very neat and helped out around the place. At night she would always sit in the same chair until the end of the eleven-o'clock news, then go off to bed, which was next to a wall in the women's section of the shelter.

Rosita slows down a bit as we approach a woman who has her back toward us. She is on her knees.

"Sherry?" Rosita calls out.

The woman turns around. "Yes?" I see a little boy sitting down as she ties his shoe.

"You seen Dorothy?"

"In the back, getting her hair did," she tells her.

Rosita looks back at me. "Gurl, you know us, we gonna stay sharp, no matter what we goin' through."

Soon enough we are inside a room that has been made into a beauty shop. There are two chairs, both with women getting their hair done. And four chairs sitting against a wall are full with ladies waiting their turn. When Rosita walks in, the ladies smile at her.

"I ain't moving this time, Ro," a lady shouts out. She looks to be about thirty and has a short haircut that is being dyed.

"Did I ask your ass to get up?" Rosita giggles. "I would be wrong as hell to do that the way you been looking 'round here, girl…"

"No, but you know how yo' ass is. Always claiming you got something to do and your hair can't wait. I was just saying if that was the case, you was waiting today with yo big ass. I don't care if you run this piece or not."

The other females along with Rosita laugh. I notice Rosita looking at a woman reading a book. She didn't even look up to see what all the commotion was about.

"Dorothy?" Rosita hollers out. "You got company." I follow Rosita over.

"Dorothy, meet…" She looks down at me.

"Lala," I tell her again.

"Yeah, Dorothy meet Lala. She's come out here to pay you a visit."

Dorothy puts down her book on her lap, then looks at me. "You came to see me?"

"Yes…"

"I don't know you? Who are you?"

"My name is Lala. I work at a youth center and I'm your son Sean's mentor."

She pauses for a second and looks up at me from her seat as if she is making the decision whether or not to admit she has a son. Then her eyes start to water a bit. "Sean?"

"Yes."

"My Sean?"

I smile at her. I can see Sean through her eyes.

"C'mon, sit down," she tells me.

And I do.

Chapter 26

I only have a short while to sit and talk with Dorothy before it's her turn to get her hair done. She asks the hairdresser to clip her ends, comb her hair back, then to place a do-rag on her head and wrap it nice and tight. It only takes Karen, the lady doing everyone's hair, a short time to handle Dorothy's request. Karen is a very fast talker, her pace forces listeners to tune in with undivided attention. I gather she has told her story to her customers more than once by the way everyone knows so much of her business. She had owned Sparkles Beauty Shop over in College Park until the IRS took it away. Her husband refused to file taxes. Then he left her shortly afterward, never letting her know he was unhappy in their relationship or that there was money due the government.

By listening to the ladies in the parlor section of the shelter, I quickly realize many of them claimed to be there by one way or another because of the choices their men made for them concerning their lives. During the conversation, I feel myself easing up on my slightly felt stereotypes of the women being in the shelter and homeless because they were lazy or selfish. I begin to understand their pain and situations. For no other reason than not being educated, I had lived my whole life believing people in shelters didn't want or didn't work to better themselves. But I was wrong. These women were hard workers, who loved life, their children, and their jobs but had been placed in situations beyond their control which landed them in the shelter. They made me realize without campaigning that everyone was a blink of an eye from joining millions of other people who had to turn to shelters for assistance. And for no other reason I am glad that I found Dorothy and had the opportunity to visit with the other ladies and get their perspective.

Dorothy agrees to walk with me the few blocks back to the coffee house. I am happy that we are finally going to sit down and talk alone. For most of the walk, she has been quiet, not a bit reflective of all the chit-chat in the parlor. But when we sit down, it is a different story altogether.

Her eyes brighten. "So, you wanted to talk to me about my son?"

I smile back 'cause the thought of Sean is so warming. "Yes, I'm his mentor."

"From the center, right?"

"Right. You know about the center?"

She nods. "Sent all my kids there before I left. Hoped that someone would take them under their wing, but my girls were back in the house before I was. The only one who wanted to stay was Sean. That boy just loves to play." Dorothy tries to smile, but her face becomes worried close to tears.

"Dorothy…"

She points at me. "Wait a second. I've been meaning to tell you. Call me Dee. I tell everyone at the shelter otherwise. I don't plan on being there forever, you know, so it's no use telling everyone my business."

"I understand, Dee," I tell her.

"So, tell me about Sean? How's he doin'?" Her face is full of hope for her son.

"Sean is wonderful and I have fallen for him!"

"But there's a problem, right?"

I nod my head.

"Well, what is it?"

"I took Sean to the zoo the other day and we were riding through downtown on the way home, and he saw you sitting at the bus stop. And it really tore him up inside."

Dee sort of whispers to herself. "Damn it." Then she takes out a small bottle of Hennessy from her purse, opens it and pours half of it into her tea. "You know, I didn't always drink. Never could stand it—the smell and all. Plus, my father used to drink every day 'til he died. It's just that this last year has been so damn rough," she explains.

I watch her mix her drink together with her spoon. "How so?"

She looks at me deeply, takes a sip, and thinks for a beat or two. "I don't know, if you really want to know…"

"I wouldn't be here, if I didn't, would I?"

"Well, it's complicated."

"No time constraints on me," I tell her.

She exhales hard. "I would never have believed in a million years, that my family would end up like this."

I don't want to push, but I am waiting for the exact time to ask her why, and she reads me like a bestseller.

"You've talked to Mark, haven't you?"

"Well, afterward. After I saw you, then Sean was uncontrollable. I told him and…"

"What'd he say?"

"I can say that he wasn't very happy that I brought up what happened and was even more upset when I told him that I went back to look for you with Sean."

She puts down her tea and sits up closer to the table. "You brought my baby back to see me?" Dee asks so nicely. I can see just the thought of Sean lights her up.

"But you were gone."

Dee takes her cup, then sips.

"So, you want to tell me what's going on, Dee?"

"It's complicated, Lala. I mean, relationships are complicated, you know?"

"Oh...you don't have to tell me. If you only knew what I've been through myself."

"Your man?"

"Umm-hmm..."

"What happened?"

I'm thinking if I don't open up to her, there is no way she is ever going to return the favor. So I am blunt before I gaze out the window as I tell her. "He dumped me for my best friend."

"Fuckin' bastard...," Dee spews out.

We both share a laugh.

"And she's a tramp," she adds.

"You got any more of that liquor left?" I want to know.

Dee reaches into her purse and pours what is left in the bottle into my cup. "Hurt much when he left?"

"Like hell," I tell her. "Never thought I would feel pain like that over him. I mean, he was the last person in this world who I thought would ever hurt me."

"Why do they do it?" Dee wants to know.

"Oh, if I knew, I would sell it." And I am serious about that.

"Girl, don't you know how rich you would be?"

"Just imagine."

"You would be on some Oprah shit."

"Please, Oprah would be calling me asking me for a loan, I would have so much money."

Dee pauses. "Just ain't right how they do us. Fill our heads up with all these dreams and aspirations, then when we buy into their bullshit, they do some shit that tears it all apart and leaves us just fucking out of our minds."

"Sometimes I wonder if it ain't just worth going at it alone."

"Yeah, but by the time we find that out, we have kids and are stuck trying to do a job that definitely takes two people to accomplish."

"You're right about that.

"You got kids?"

Her question kind of hurts so I wash down the negative thoughts with my drink before I'm able to answer. "No, I don't have any. But he certainly does."

"With her…?"

I confirm with an embarrassed nod.

"Trifling pair, hunh?"

"Nasty."

"Don't sweat it, Sweetie. Maybe you're lucky 'cause that's when my life became complicated."

"How so?"

"Well, my girls are adopted. We adopted all three of them when my doctor was sure I couldn't get pregnant. Then all of sudden…guess who pops up pregnant." Dee smiles.

"Amazing."

"You telling me? So, there we were. Mark was ecstatic, the girls helped as much as they could, and then Sean was born."

"So what happened? How did things change?"

Dee looks at me hard verifying to herself that she can

trust me. Her contemplation lasts so long that I am getting ready to settle for her not telling me anything at all.

"One day I came back from the mall with Sean and my two youngest girls, and when I walk into our bedroom, Mark is in the bed with my oldest daughter, Keisha."

I am speechless.

"I've never told anyone this," Dee confides. "And the look on your face is the reason why," she explains.

"I'm just shocked," I tell her.

"You? I must have thrown up a hundred times that night. I couldn't even ask Keisha about it until at least three months afterward."

"So, was it a mutual thing?"

She shakes her head no. "Mark had been threatening her. Telling Keisha that he would send her and her sisters back to the agency if she didn't keep her mouth shut and do exactly what he told her."

"Now…he's a bastard," I realize.

"But there's more. Mark has had sex with all the girls. Telling them all the same thing."

I'm just about at tears now. "How old are they all?"

"Keisha's fifteen, Darmina is thirteen, and the baby girl Shelly, just turned eleven."

"And you never told anyone about this?"

Dee's eyes begin to water. "I just couldn't. He's my husband."

"I know but…"

"At first he would do these things when no one else

was home. But lately he hasn't cared. He hasn't cared about shit and he's sleeping with them any time of the day and doesn't give a damn who in the house knows about it. But they sure better not say a word. It's like everyone in that house is his for the taking." Dee begins to break down. I place my hand over hers trying to give her some comfort.

Chapter 27

I call Lorenzo and tell him I have some pressing news to share. He insists that I come over to his house because he's cooking dinner and doesn't want to eat alone.

"How do you know she's telling the truth?" is the first thing out of Lorenzo's mouth after I tell him what I found out about Sean's family.

When he challenges me, I cop a bit of an attitude. "Why would she lie?"

"Why wouldn't she?"

"What the hell, Lorenzo?"

"Look, I have to play the devil's advocate. I've seen some hellacious allegations that never materialize, and I just don't understand why she would leave them in the situation when she is pretending to care so damn much about them?"

"She said, the only reason she left is because she doesn't have a job. Mark has the job. She's never worked since they've been together, so she's like ass out right now."

"And I bet she never told the kids why she left?"

"She says, the girls probably have an idea because she talked to them before she left. Told them what was going on was wrong and she couldn't handle it but would be back for them all. But Sean doesn't; he's completely out the loop on this one. He's just too young to understand."

"Doesn't seem right to me…," Lorenzo insists.

"Why not?"

"Just doesn't and I don't have any other reason than that."

"Well, this type of shit happens, you know?"

"How do you know the girls aren't in this with him? Some of these girls are lightning fast, Lala."

"So what? What if they are experimenting? Does it make it right for their guardian to take advantage of them? Of course not."

Lorenzo pauses and takes a deep breath. "I don't know what you want me to do, Lala."

"I don't, either," I tell him. "I mean, intervene or some shit. Hasn't the center ever stepped up to help kids?"

"Of course," he says.

"When? What happened?"

"Before I came on board, there was a counselor who thought one of his kids was being beaten at home after the kid swore to him it was happening."

"So what happened?"

"The center looked into it. Tried to get the kid taken from his parent, then got sued to be damned because the kid lied, and we went after the kid's mother with everything we had. Cost the association so much money they damn near shut our branch down."

"Well, something has to be done. Those kids already lost their real parents, and if I sit back and let it continue to happen, I'm as much to blame as their sorry-ass so-called father."

We go back and forth for about thirty minutes, and I defer because Lorenzo has dealt with these types of allegations before. I decide to trust his wisdom and leave it alone after he promises that he will call a lawyer to see what he recommends. Just knowing that I would be able to get back with Dee and give her some options soothed my mind for a moment, but I wasn't going to let it go. I truly felt sad for her.

"So, this is your bachelor pad?" I ask Lorenzo while I finally look around. It's kind of cute inside. He lives in an older house but it has character. For some reason, I fall in love with the brick walls on the corner of the room where we are sitting. We are in a television room not far from the kitchen where Lorenzo has been cooking what smells like spaghetti or something else with a pleasant Italian aroma. His furniture isn't cutting-edge contemporary flair but it's still in style. He can probably get away with another few years of use before it's apparent that it needs to go. I enjoy looking at the hardwood floors he has in every room. The wood is dark but shiny, almost like glass. His apartment has an earth-toned, warm, masculine feel. I realize it's definitely a reflection of his style of wardrobe and the beaded necklaces and bracelets he wears.

He offers a glass of wine. I accept and ask for some of what he is cooking because a sista is feeling the hunger pangs for real.

On his way to the kitchen, he turns to me. "Tell me something first."

"What is it?"

"Can you still call this a bachelor pad if you've been dateless for over six months?"

"Six months?"

"I know, embarrassing, right?"

"For a man…in Atlanta? Yeah, that's kind of…"

"Oh, it's like that? Well, anyway, I made spaghetti."

I sip my wine, a Red Zinfandel chilled just right. "I'm just sharing the facts with you, my brother."

"Well, what can I say? I'm just a choosy mother-fucker."

"And there's a lot in the tank for men to choose from here in Atlanta."

"Sometimes the pickings aren't that good, though," he tells me.

"Meaning?"

"Meaning it's a mental thing with me. I have to be mental with a person in tune so much that it's like walking in their spirit."

"That's interesting…"

"You think?"

"I do, but after you're strolling in the spirit, what makes you so sure you won't want to stop walking with the person altogether like most men do?" I just can't refuse to ask him since it was what Keith did to me.

"Most men?" Lorenzo repeats.

I smile at him. "Yeah, I said it."

"Put it like this. I'm not 'most men'."

"Oh, excuse me," I say with a laughing edge. "How'd we get on this topic, anyway?"

I am not going to lie. Lorenzo can cook, at least spaghetti, and I don't care what he thinks about my eating portions after I ask for a second helping.

We are relaxing in his TV room and he plops in a tape of *Love Jones* which is a classic in itself. We both know the movie very well, yet the characters are able to pull us in and we share our views on what they all were going through.

Lorenzo confides that he is sort of a movie buff and he shares that he thinks Isaiah Washington is a hell of an actor who has gotten a bad break on *Grey's Anatomy*. I let him know that I am waiting on Larenz Tate and Nia Long to finally get theirs, too. We both are partial to Bill Bellamy and disagree with the media's portrayal of Lisa Nicole Carson being nasty and rude. In my opinion she is so talented and the original *Sex in the City* girl.

I must admit I was having a nice time. But somewhere in between eating and watching the movie, I began to think about Sean. I was wondering what he was up to and if he was all right because he was carrying a hell of a burden; some of which he didn't even know about. I rationalized that his father, Mark, more than likely was somewhere standing over him like a bully telling him to "man up" and stop being a punk over the situation of seeing his mother on the corner. I wouldn't have had a problem with that if he was talking about a small bump on Sean's head. But this was the boy's mother; and he missed her so.

After a while, my focus has drifted way off the movie and I take my arms and draw them into my body tightly as if I am cold. Lorenzo is sitting next to me and notices. He cautiously places his arm around me and assures me that Sean will be okay. It was nice of him and I enjoy the fact he knew what I was thinking without having to say anything again.

Chapter 28

It's been exactly eight days since I last talked with Sydney so I call him and he answers. It's genuinely good to hear his voice. He always has a way of making me feel safe and I know if I ever run into trouble; he is the man to see. He definitely proved that to me when he stepped up to take care of Keith. Even though it was wrong to even go there, I appreciated him for that and all the honesty he always shared. From the sounds in the background, I can tell he's sitting in the club. While we catch up, I imagine his distinguished face and dapper clothes draping perfectly on his lean body like he is in the mob or something.

"I've been calling you," he tells me in a prying, "wanting to know if I was okay" kind of way.

I look down at my answering machine sitting on my nightstand. "Why didn't you leave a message?"

"I called at work, tried to surprise you."

"Oh, work…"

"Yeah, the place where you make your chips." He laughs and changes his tone a bit before he says, "The dollar, dollar bills, ya'll…"

"Well, I'm kinda not there at the moment."

"Not there? What happened? You get laid off?"

"Took a leave of absence," I'm kind of embarrassed to tell him.

Sydney doesn't respond right back.

I rush to get the words out of my mouth so that he can. "I just couldn't stand seeing Adria in the office and hearing about her baby," I tell him. "My leave just started."

"Oh, Ms. Thang's back, hunh?"

"Unfortunately."

Sydney's voice perks up a bit. "Maybe it'll be a good thing if you meet my wife, after all."

At that moment I'm glad that Sydney can't see me because I have my hand over my mouth. I have totally forgotten about his request of meeting his wife. His request was so far off the wall to me that I had pushed it out of my mind.

"About that, Sydney," I stumble, trying to find the words.

"It would be good for you, Lala. I never told you, but she's head of human resources at CMN."

"Your wife?"

"You don't believe me?""

"I didn't say that, it's just that…you never mentioned it before."

"I didn't have a reason to. Now, I do, so there it is."

I go back quickly and remind myself that Sydney didn't tell me what kind of friends he had, either until he thought I might want to use their services. "Just so many facets, hunh, Mr. Sydney…," I toyed.

"Well, you know," he says in his street tone. "I've learned you never show your entire hand."

For some reason I put pressure on myself to give Sydney an answer right away instead of sitting down and trying to be rational about the whole introduction thing. It just strikes me as very odd that his wife would want to talk to me. No doubt about it, when I first met Sydney, he was mysterious and someone I needed for the moment. But not once have I ever thought I couldn't believe what he has ever told me. He is definitely a man of his word, so I make up my mind on pure guts. He is waiting on me on the phone to agree to the meeting.

"Okay, why not, Sydney? I'll meet your wife. I mean you can never meet enough important people, right?"

"Good, I'll set everything up," he assures me.

"She's not upset with me…right? Going out having dinner with her man and all?"

"Lala, you don't have to worry."

"I have to tell you I do have some apprehensions about meeting her. You understand, don't you?

"I can tell you, unequivocally, she doesn't mean you any harm. Nancy is so delightful, it would be good for her, I think."

"What do you mean?"

"Just to see you. Talk with you…get some things cleared up that she might be thinking."

"See, this is what I don't understand."

"About our relationship, Lala," Sydney tries to explain.

"Whose relationship?"

"More than likely the one I have with her and the one I have with you." Sydney's tone is so nonchalant that I quickly ease up.

"Girl talk, I guess."

"So when and where will this all take place?"

"That's the message I've been leaving on your machine. Dinner tomorrow at six."

Chapter 29

The next moment in my life is definitely confusing. I mean, what's in the closet to wear, in order to meet the wife of a man you damned near slept with, but on the flip side, you've turned into pretty good friends with. I decide to go silky casual. A tan silk dress with a pair of my Jimmy Choo shoes. Sydney had reserved a table for us at The Dish in Buckhead and I didn't know if I should be fashionably late or twenty minutes early.

I arrive right on time. So does she. We don't know at the time, but we are standing right next to each other as we wait to be seated. We're looking out into the restaurant for a woman sitting alone at a table. I am seated first, and just like Sydney suggested, I tell my waiter my name and let him know I am waiting for a guest.

I did notice how gorgeous Nancy was while we were standing waiting to be seated. In fact, I was very close to asking her the name of the beautician who had hooked her hair up. When we are finally seated, then meet and greet, I realize she is a very stunning woman. She is artistic-like, very beamy and elegant but graceful enough that I didn't feel as though she thought she was better than anyone else sitting in the restaurant. I know Sydney is in his fifties, knocking real close to sixty. But Nancy looks much younger…ten to fifteen years younger. Her face is flawless. I imagine she drinks the prescribed amount of water a body needs her entire life. She is the perfect example of "black don't crack." Her skin tone looks like a perfectly made cube of caramel candy. I enjoy the fact that she is quaint and very fashionable. She is so graceful when she first sits down and extends her hand to me. The tennis bracelets dangling from both wrists and the rock Sydney has placed on her finger make her freshly done nails stand out even more.

After we introduce ourselves, our conversation is off and running. We share everything from our childhood, families, schooling, college. When Nancy mentions that Sydney told her that I had been writing in top-market television for close to eight years, she seems very much interested in why I took a leave of absence. We have our share of daiquiris, so it is way too late for me to try to be politically correct about the situation. I tell her every trifling detail of the drama that landed my man together with my girlfriend and now *their* child, and how I met her husband.

"So, do you blame her for what happened?" Nancy wants to know.

I just about have my daiquiri up to my lips. "Are you

kidding me? Of course I do. And his ass, too," I tell her. "Over six years is a hell of an investment."

"That's a pretty good stretch but try knowing someone over half your life."

"Wow, that's unbelievable." I chuckle a bit.

"What...?"

"It just dawned on me that you're the first person I've ever met that has been together with their mate longer than the time I spent with my ex."

"Well, I tell you one thing. With everything happening these days, be thankful for the six years."

"Thankful? It's like I wasted my time," I tell her. It was exactly the way I felt. It was Nancy's time to crack a smile at me. "Don't you feel the same way?"

"Look, Sweetie, it's better to count your losses now. You don't want to ride down the road of decades with a man, then find out when you're my age, he feels it's time for a little space. Shoot, space for what? That wide window of life we used to have is shutting faster than he may know," Nancy offers.

"So you're talking about this whole openness thing Sydney told me about?"

"Exactly..."

I have to cut her off before she goes any further. "Look, Nancy, I never..."

"Gurl, you don't have to explain yourself to me. Shit, my man is fine. Finest man I ever knew in my life. The first day I ever saw him in my life, I knew I was gonna marry him. Do whatever it takes to get him; and that's exactly what I did. So you don't have to explain anything. That man has skills," she boasts.

"Yeah, he's very suave," I confirm with much respect. "But I thought you were in agreement with him on this *open* issue?"

"There's another attribute Sydney has, but I can't stand it," she says. "He's so damn convincing. Have you found that out about him?"

"I'm sitting here, aren't I?"

We share a silly moment, then Nancy continues filling me in.

"When I first met Sydney there wasn't anybody who could tell me he wasn't a free soul. He was made that way. His mother and father separated early and he was an only child. He doesn't talk about it much because it's too depressing."

"I'm sure," I say. Getting this background on Sydney is really interesting to me. It is like I could put paint on some of the numbers that are blank from what I know of him, so I listen intently.

"So, being independent afforded Sydney to do a lot of things when he was younger that he shouldn't have had to do as a boy growing into a man. But on the flip side, though, some of the things he did made him a strong man who is very truthful, even when what he has to say hurts him to feel it or say it."

"So, his free soul pulls at him?"

"Exactly. Let me tell you one thing about men," she says.

I smile. "Only one?"

She smiles back. "They really aren't shit."

"Okay…"

"But the truth of the matter is—and I would debate it with any one of these *woman's lib-don't-need-a-man-for-nothing heifers because they're all so strong*—we need men in our life. I'm a little more down the street than you are, and I know how it is to think you can pick up and start over and have your whole life in front of you after you break up with a man."

"Shit, I don't feel like that. I have to have kids and soon," I tell her.

"Understood. But the truth of the matter is, I need a man in my life. It's always been like that for me. It started off with my father when I was a little girl. Just to see him after school when he came home from work and to sit and talk with him. He always seemed to be attentive to me, listen to everything I wanted to say to him on purpose. As I became older, he told me to make sure any man that I might end up with was just as pleasing as he had been to me." Nancy pauses. "And Sydney for years had been that man."

"And now?"

"Oh, he still is. But when he shared with me that he wanted to explore this open-ended relationship, I agreed with him because I thought it was a phase. I thought he would come to his senses and realize the investment we both had made to each other. But so far, he hasn't."

"So, how long has this been going on?"

"About two years. He told me he just wanted to have another voice to listen to sometimes. Said that it was becoming difficult for him to be with me but not because he didn't love me anymore."

"But you agreed to this thing, right?"

"I did. Even fought with his idea myself for a while. I mean, having dinner with another man was imaginable. And just being able to think about it was enough for me to realize that years with someone does something to you. It makes you look at what is, what could be, and wonder what will be while you are really still trying to find out what makes this person tick. That's why I wanted to meet you. I wanted to find out what kind of person you were. Wanted to see why there was a glow in my man's eyes again."

"Trust me, Nancy. Sydney and I are strictly friends," I assure her.

"I know that. Even if all the conditions were right for you two to make love, he wouldn't find his self to do it," Nancy says. "Sydney respects me too much. But I think just knowing that he could, really gets that negro off." She laughs.

At this point I don't know what to say, but I feel closer to Nancy and respect her. "He'll come around," I tell her. "Maybe this is just a phase?"

"I understand and have tried patiently to ride it out, but phase or not, I have thought about this long and hard enough. I'm fed up with trying to lick his wounds while I get gangrene because of mine."

"What do you mean?"

"I'm saying that I need Sydney in my life as he has always been—and if I can't have him that way, I think it's time for me to move in another direction, no matter how difficult it may be at this point in my life."

Chapter 30

The adjustment period of living without Keith in my life still hasn't permeated one-hundred percent. The reality of not being together anymore has sunk in, but totally adapting to taking on major issues alone is definitely taking some time getting used to. Life is tricky, if not downright deceiving. Who would have believed that six months earlier, I would be deeply involved trying to get myself back on track after a break-up, attempting to reunite a mother with her family, and to top it off, in a position to have to tell a man that I almost slept with that his wife is seriously thinking about leaving his ass? Stress that I had not been used to was building. I really didn't know how to take all of the sudden intrusions in my life. I had been drama free with Keith; at least unknowingly until I realized life was more complicated than the only issues I believed I had while I lived with him. The funny thing about it; they all had to be dealt with.

I had only hoped that Sean would be at the center the next time I visited. It's been close to two weeks and I haven't spoken with him since Mark had been so forceful with me concerning Dee. I felt I should ease any tension that may be lingering in the household due to my intervention, so I initially, for the sake of Sean, left well enough alone.

It is around eleven on a Saturday morning, there are a lot of kids running throughout the center enjoying their time to play. Most of them are having the best time with the new arts and crafts that have been brought in. I am on my way to Lorenzo's office and I hear Sean call my name.

I bend down to give him a hug. "Hey, man!"

He returns a tight, loving hug. There's no doubt he has missed me as much as I've missed him. "Where you been?" he asks without hesitation.

"Aww, honey, I've been a little busy lately, but I've been really thinking about you," I let him know.

"Why haven't you called me?"

It is so damn hard to lie to kids—at least for me. "I just thought I'd give you a little time to spend with your family. How's everything?"

"Fine…"

"You sure?"

"Yes." He smiles. "Guess what? My dog came back home."

"Really? That's wonderful."

"But he's gone again," he says.

"Gone…?"

"Yup, he left. He stayed with me one day and the next

day he ran out the house again when my sister opened the door."

"Well, I'm sure he'll be back."

Sean thinks for a while, then smiles.

"So how are your sisters?"

Sean steps back a bit, then looks at the ground.

"How are they doin'? Everyone's okay?" I try to find out.

"My daddy told me not to talk about them."

Sean's whole demeanor has changed. Almost as though the thought of his sisters draws the air out of him. I kneel down at his level and reach out to him for another hug. "Well, if that's what he told you, that's fine with me, okay?

It takes Sean longer than normal to answer. He is pouting a bit.

I reinforce what I said to him with a smile while looking directly in his eyes.

"Okay?"

He smiles, then hugs me again. "Okay."

"Listen, why don't you go play and I will come out in a while and maybe shoot some hoops with you," I tell him.

"You wanna shoot some ball with me, Ms. Lala?"

"Sure do…"

"Okay, I'll go get a ball and go practice. How 'bout some Twenty-one?"

I give him a kiss on his cheek. "You got it."

I watch him run to get a ball, then continue to

Lorenzo's office. Seeing Sean is emotional for me. In my mind the only thing children should have to worry about is just being children. Play, have fun, movies, candy, and holidays. Life situations occur, but damn, leave the children out of it. Let them be. Let adults deal. With all the pressing thoughts on my mind, I realize I'm in sort of a daze when I walk into Lorenzo's office.

"You must have seen the young'n," he says.

"How'd you know?"

"All over your face."

"Boy, shouldn't have to deal with it, Lorenzo."

"I know. Shit, life is hard."

"Much too difficult." I sit down in a chair across from Lorenzo's desk. He's standing fooling around with the window directly behind his desk. "What are you doing?"

"Fuckin' window is stuck," he says. "I would complain…"

"To who?"

He laughs. "That's my point." Lorenzo tries a few more times to open the window. "Fuck it," he surrenders, then sits down. "We'll just burn up together."

Right off the bat I want to know if he'd contacted legal about what we could do to try to intervene in Sean's and his mother's situation. Lorenzo is uncomfortable because he just worked out. It's much too hot in his office, so we go outside to catch a breeze and talk.

"Now, that's better." He exhales and wipes his forehead.

Outside the center is another full-length court, some picnic tables, and swings for the kids. We sit down at a concrete picnic table under a shade tree.

When we are comfortable, I ask about the lawyer again and he gives me all the information I need. I'm surprised when Lorenzo lets me know that he has set up a meeting with them the very next day. Lorenzo begs me not to get too excited because it would be a definite fight to get legal to agree with drawing up the paperwork so we could bring the police in to investigate. But I don't care and already have in my mind that everything will work out for the best.

"So…," Lorenzo says. He is tearing apart a fall leaf that has found its way on our table. "How have you been?"

My first instinct is to tell Lorenzo about the meeting I had with Nancy and how we met. But I force myself to stay quiet about it just because I think it would be too much like letting him in. "I'm good," I tell him.

"You know, I had a nice time with you the other night."

I smile at him. "I'm glad, Lorenzo. Thanks again for the grub."

He chuckles a bit. "That's it?"

I don't understand his playful sarcasm. I feel my eyes squinting trying to understand.

"If you hadn't noticed, I'm trying desperately to get my flirt on."

"Oh…" I put my hand over my mouth. "Is that what you're doing?"

"Yes…I was throwing it out there and you didn't even catch it," he teases.

"I'm sorry. Do your thang then, boy," I entice and go with the flow.

"Can't do it now. I would feel like a fool, a complete sucker," he jokes.

I turn to the basketball court when I hear a ball bouncing. It's Sean all by his lonesome trying to get the ball up to the hoop. "Okay, your choice," I tell Lorenzo. "Hey, I gotta go. I promised Sean a game of basketball." I stand up from the table and kind of dread the short walk in the sun to the court.

"Well, how about dinner?" Lorenzo wants to know.

"You want to take me to dinner?"

"Sure, I do."

I look over at Sean and he has stopped bouncing the ball. He's looking over at me with the ball under his arm.

"Sure, I'll go to dinner with you," I tell Lorenzo. Then I am off and running to the court to put a hurting on Sean.

It doesn't take Sean long to become bored with playing ball. He scores two baskets and the next thing I know we are playing dodgeball and laughing up a storm. I am forced to take a break because a sister has lost all the oxygen in her being, so I lead Sean over to the set of swings and we both take a seat.

"Me and my mom did this once," Sean tells me.

"Really?

"Uh..huh…" He is nodding his head up and down like he never wants to forget.

I look at Sean's little chocolate face and smile. I think to myself if I ever would have a son, I would want him to have as much life and passion as the precious boy I am sitting right next to. "When was that?"

"Right before she left," he says in such a way that there is no hiding she is laying heavily on his mind.

I pause for a moment. "You know your mother really loves you, Sean."

"I know," he says.

"And she really cares about you and your sisters."

"I know," he says again.

"And one day you'll all be together again."

"I know…"

Sean is crying again and I'm hating every second of it. I am hurting so much that I become a little angry over the entire situation. I pull out my cell phone and dial the shelter. Dee is dispatched to the phone and when she answers, I give Sean the phone. "Here, baby, someone wants to talk to you."

He looks at me confused but takes the phone, anyway. "Hello?" His face lights up as soon as he hears Dee's voice. "Mama…is this really you?"

The whole moment is too much for me to take, so I rub Sean on his head while he's going a mile a minute with Dee. I walk away, so I can shed a few tears of my own.

Chapter 31

I leave the center feeling a little better. Sean has a smile on his face and is more at ease because he's actually heard his mother's voice. I feel as though I am moving in the right direction in getting them back together, especially after knowing the appointment with legal is Monday morning at nine o'clock sharp. I have plans to meet Lorenzo for dinner at seven at the Spaghetti Warehouse, but I call Sydney to see if he could meet me anywhere close to downtown so I can fill him in on his wife. We decide to meet in the Underground.

"So you two broke bread?" Sydney wants to know first thing. We are both enjoying the sax player who seems to have everyone's attention in the main walkway.

"Yes, we had a nice time. You know Nancy is very nice, Sydney."

"Without a doubt," he admits.

"And very beautiful, too."

I am very blunt with him because I had a moment to think about our meeting. I realize that she really loves this man. But somehow in the time they've been together, it seems as though Sydney is the half of the relationship that has drifted apart. I want to find out why, so I ask. In Sydney's defense, he does try to answer truthfully and searches for the truth a few times.

"Please don't call it a mid-life crisis…"

"I'm not."

"I mean I know things happen, but you can tell just by talking to Nancy that she deeply cares for you."

"I love her, too," he replies. "That has never been the issue."

"Well, help me to understand. She told me that she only went along with this *open* relationship you guys have going on because you're the one who wanted it."

"It's true. I initiated the arrangement."

"But *why* is the question?" I joke a bit. "I am so damn happy you didn't take me up on my offer that night, Sydney… Shit, it would have floored her."

"She told you that?"

"No. Why? You haven't…"

"No, I haven't been with anyone, Lala. Geez, I can see she's won you over and the girls are bonding."

"Look, I'm all for a stable relationship. If you haven't forgotten, I would still be in one if my ex had felt the same."

"It's time, Lala. It has slipped away and here we are."

"I thought time makes a relationship better?"

"What happens when it can't get any better? That's the question?"

"That's terrible, Sydney…"

"What am I supposed to do? I'm telling you the truth."

"Well, have you talked to her about it?"

"Yes, I've tried to explain it the best way I can."

"And that's how the openness agreement came about?"

"Exactly."

I didn't want to come out and be the messenger of bad news, so I stay quiet until Sydney looks and realizes there is something very important I need to tell him. When he does, I say, "She's thinking about divorce, Sydney."

He doesn't respond. Just swipes his face and tries to force himself to get in to the sax player and his now blue solo. To me his face looks as though it is relieved but in pain at the same time. I don't know what else to say to him. I told him what he wanted to know and now it is up to him if he wants to make things right with his wife. I'm not capable of understanding how Sydney feels about his wife. I understand love, though. I understand that when a woman loves a man with all her heart and soul, *time* is just something that passes by without interference of love shared. I am forced to remember back when I would try to go through life stages and how they would be with Keith. Marriage. Baby. Family. I ran the whole gamut of life, did it quite often when I would drift away. I never thought that *time* would be a crutch in our relationship. To me, *time* was strength. It made sense, it was what made a relationship. Up until I met

Nancy, the only reason I remotely understood Sydney was probably because I was hurting.

But this *time* thing, at the moment I couldn't feel what he was saying to me. *Time* I could not buy into because *time* was strength to me.

Sydney's voice is lower than I have ever heard it before now. "A divorce, hunh?"

"That's what she said. And I think it's uncalled for. You two have been through too much."

Sydney doesn't respond.

"I tell you one thing, though. You need to make it work. You do want it to work, Sydney?"

Sydney takes a deep breath. "I dunno. I can't help how I feel, can I?"

"No one can. Maybe you need someone to talk to about this besides me?"

"I'm like the majority of black folk. I don't trust no shrink, Lala."

"You ever been to one?"

"No. You?"

"No…"

"Well, you see my point then."

"I would go, in this case. I think you need to fight to keep what you've established. Wow, I couldn't even imagine wanting to throw something away after so long."

"I really don't. Make no mistake about it."

"Well, work it out then."

Chapter 32

It's seven when I meet Lorenzo. He calls to let me know he would drive. He picks me up downtown. When we make our connection in front of the Underground, he's holding one long-stemmed rose. He says it's symbolic for our very first official date. Impressive. His mother must have taught him well because when we get into his sparkling, black, souped-up Mustang, he opens and shuts the door for me. Jazz is playing in the CD changer and there's a light hint of strawberry scent floating around.

While we drive, Lorenzo is full of questions. He wants to know where I was for a second time, but the conversation is much more intimate. He asks what I did when I was in high school, college, my interests, hobbies, and future plans. It has been so long since I'd been out with anyone since Keith that even though I know Lorenzo, it is a bit much opening up to him. He jokes about it and tells me it's okay because it's natural for a woman to be guarded after a breakup from such a long relationship. Lorenzo starts talking when he can get a word in. But the conversation isn't about him. *Thank God*. He has topics of discussion that interest me and make me feel comfortable. His smooth conversation lasts the entire night. I can't lie; we have a very nice time at the restaurant. And to my surprise, afterward we go bowling and then for drinks.

Lorenzo impresses me and I tell him so. He asks if I would like to go to his place afterward but I decline. I have business to take care of in the morning at the lawyer's office. The best thing about my decision is he understands completely.

The next morning I try not to look so hyped and anxious, but I am. To finally talk to someone who could help me get Sean, along with his sisters, back together with Dee and away from that bastard Mark, was motivating in itself. While I wait on counsel in a conference room, I cannot erase the look on Sean's face while he speaks to his mother on the phone.

I turn toward the conference room doors when I hear them swing open. My mouth is stuck open and my head begins to spin like a turbo-charged turbine because I cannot believe my eyes. This results in a rushing, burning sensation in my body and it's damn near uncontrollable. I am at a loss for understanding anything. As Keith plops his heavy-duty Kenneth Cole briefcase on the shiny maple table, the echo that only occurs in large rooms brings me back to a somewhat stable condition. We both say each other's names at the same time.

"What are you doing here?" I say first with plenty of attitude.

"I work here," he says back. "What are *you*...doing here?"

"I am here to see a lawyer about a potential case."

"Well, guess I'm the lawyer," he decides.

"So, what are you doing here?" I ask again.

He gradually begins to reach into his brief. "I already told you, I work here."

I am shaking my head desperately trying to understand. "No, no. Why are you working here? What happened to your partnership? I thought you made partner."

I am beside myself and full of anger to see the smile that I used to adore and love so much. "We bought this place out. And I'm running things here now. You know, going back and forth," he says.

I was never a money-hungry woman. But I begin counting in my head how much money he is making now. Fuckin' bastard.

Keith has made his way over to the other side of the table. He sits directly in front of me, in the most expensive suit I have ever seen on his body. Nobody can tell me he isn't finally getting paid.

He straightens out his tie. "So, what can I do for you?"

Telling him to kiss my caramel-colored, cellulite-forming ass is a thought. But I struggle to open my mouth and hold a conversation with his backstabbing, baby-making, punk ass. This isn't about me. I calm myself. "I'm here about the Youth Center."

"Oh yeah," he says. Then he looks up at me for less than a second. "So when did you start working there?"

"I don't," I tell him.

"Then why are you here?"

"I'm a mentor. My intentions were to keep young boys from turning into men who break commitments and lie. So far, so good."

"Oh…okay." Keith keeps his eyes on the paperwork he has in front of him.

I wait for him to say something, but he just continues to read. "So?"

He puts his index finger up to me. That alone pisses me off. Then he closes his folder shut and stands up. "Well, thanks for the heads-up on this, but there are absolutely no merits on this potential case. There's no way we are going to let the Youth Center get involved in a witch hunt. Lala, it was really good to see you again," he tells me.

Keith barely looks into my eyes when he speaks, then begins to walk away. I am about to lose it. "Wait one gotdamn minute, Keith!" I'm sure everyone in the building hears the echo from my voice. I don't care and can see his shoulders drop. "That's right, take a deep breath, and tell me why this won't work?"

He turns around and straightens out his tie. "Lawsuit, you ever heard of that?"

"Yeah, I have," I say back.

"Well, that's exactly what we'll be looking at if we go take this man's kids on the grounds that his drunk runaway wife accuses him of child molestation."

"The mother isn't a drunk," I tell him.

"Says it in her file. Plus, this office did a case about a year ago when I wasn't here…"

"Yeah, yeah. I already heard about that, but it still doesn't change the fact that a crime is being committed and someone needs to intervene."

"Look, I understand what you're saying. No one likes to see this shit, but for a law firm to basically stand as accusers with the center, it just can't fly."

"That's bullshit, Keith, and you know it."

"No, Lala, it's the facts and the way it's going to be," he says. Keith turns around again and starts to walk away.

His answer…his attitude…his presence…just seeing his face again pisses me off. "Is that all you have to say to me?" Keith only has a few more steps before he opens the door. "Gotdamn it, Keith, I'm talking to your sorry ass!"

He stops this time and turns around slow but with a definite attitude. "What now, Lala?"

"What now?"

"That's right?" Keith puts his left hand in his pocket. "Don't you even care how I've been doing? That's 'what now.' How the fuck can you come in here, stand in your designer suit, and look at me and ask me 'what now'? Negro, have you gone crazy?"

"Look…"

"No, you look… You need to tell me two things. I want to know what other possibilities I have with getting this family back together and the father held responsible. And two, did your sorry ass ever love me?"

Keith looks around the conference room as though he can't believe what is going on. "Okay, okay, look. You can go to the police and see what they say. I'm telling you now, they're going to be as careful as we are." Then he exhales. "And yes, I did love you, Lala." Keith turns around and right before he touches the door to open it, he turns back around. "Oh yeah, by the way… You don't have to worry about making any more payments on the house. I've got it covered. Matter of fact, in another three months, it will be all yours." Keith stands still as though I should thank him or something. Then he speaks again. This time his voice is much lower. "It was Adria's idea. You deserve it and I agree with her," he says. Keith looks back at me one last time and then walks away.

Chapter 33

While meeting with Keith I receive two messages. The first is from Dee, who wants to make sure I am still coming to the shelter to see her. The other is from Nancy, who asks that I give her a call. I decide to drive to the shelter first. That way I can clear my head and try to forget about the surprise of seeing Keith and the reality of that bastard telling me that I can't do something that is very important to me.

The lunchtime crowd is dispersing from the cafeteria when I walk into the shelter. I spot Dee standing behind a table holding a dish rag. I swear I am trying to hide the disappointment on my face as I approach her, but I can tell that she senses things didn't go well. I promise myself before I say a word to her that I would never call anyone and get their hopes up again until I know for certain things will turn out positive. After I confirm the fact, I follow Dee into a makeshift chapel that has about four benches, an altar with a Bible sitting nearby, and a very old, almost rotten piano that has seen its best days fifty years ago. To top things off, there is a painting of a black Jesus who looks more like a pimp than our savior.

"Hope you don't mind sitting in here?" Dee says.

After a few minutes of sitting and smelling the faint smell of alcohol and God knows whatever else, I realize why she asked.

She says, "I come in here to get away sometime. You know, to lay down my burdens."

"I understand," I tell her.

"So, what's next? Did they at least tell you what our options were?"

I just nod my head.

"What's wrong, Lala? You act like you done saw the ugliest monster ever created…"

"I did. My ex," I let her know.

"That will do it every time," Dee confirms.

"He is the new counsel for the center."

"Now that's irony, isn't it?"

"Who you telling? Complete insanity."

"And no help at all?"

"He said, if we go to the police, they'll hear us out but they'll step lightly because of the fact you left the house and have been going to treatment for alcohol abuse."

"How'd they find that out?" Dee wants to know.

"I don't know, maybe it's put into some type of database when you sign up. Nothing's fuckin' private anymore." I look up to the black Jesus and tell him I am sorry.

Dee faintly laughs. "Don't worry about him. He's heard it all," she says.

While we share a downcast chuckle together, a man opens the door to the chapel and steps inside. He hesitates before he comes completely in but gathers himself and goes down to the altar and places his face in his hands.

Dee whispers, "So what do we do next?"

"I really didn't have a backup plan," I let her know.

"I don't know how long I can stay here, Lala." She nods to the man kneeling at the altar. "These folks are working my last nerves. I don't belong here."

"I know you don't, Dee," I assure her. "Nobody does."

"But as strange as it seems, it's better than being home and witnessing what's happening to the girls. I just can't go back there."

The mention of what is going on combined with Keith's refusal of getting his firm involved infuriates me even more. I hate myself that I filled Dee's head up with getting someone to back her up so that she could ultimately move back in her house and take care of her kids. Right before I am about to tell Dee that everything will be okay, the man at the altar stands to his feet, turns around, then swipes the tears from his face. He looks as though at one time in his life, he might have held some type of responsibility at a bank or something.

"Oh, Dorothy, I didn't see you there," he says.

Dee and I look at each other knowing the man saw us when he walked in.

"What is it, Stanley…." Dee sings, noticeably irate with him.

"Well, I wanted to tell you, I wanted to tell you that

I answered a call for you this morning on the pay phone."

"Really? From who?"

It is clear as day that the white man who weighs about two-hundred and fifty pounds and is balding is drunk out of his wits.

"Uh, it was from a man. I do remember that. Yeah, it was a man."

Dee is frustrated and punches her hands in her lap. "So, what did he say, Stanley?"

"See, now that's when things get a little fucked up for me," Stanley says. Then he looks at the picture of Jesus on the wall. "You think Jesus is really black?"

Dee shouts, "Who gives a damn, Stanley! Tell me what the guy said on the phone. Did he mention anything whatsoever about a job?"

"Ahhh," Stanley remembers.

Dee starts talking to him like a child. "Did…he… leave…a…number…Stanley?"

"Yeah, he sure did. He gave me his number." Stanley faintly smiles. Happy that he has remembered.

Dee puts her hand out. "Good, well, let me have the number," Dee tells him.

"What number?"

"The number to call him back!"

"I didn't write it down. I thought I could remember it." Stanley snickers. "But look at me. I'm fucked up," he says as he tiptoes past us and out the door.

Right then and there I realize that there is no way Dee is going to get things right living in the shelter.

"Go get your things," I tell her.

"What?"

"Pack up. You're going home with me," I let her know.

"I just can't go home with you?"

"Why not?"

Dee is silent.

"You can and you will. As a matter of fact, your kids are coming too."

Chapter 34

The clock in my car reads two-thirty in the afternoon. I am sitting with Dee in front of her house wondering how we should go about getting the kids and taking them over to my place. Initially, the plan I lay out for Dee seems so simple. *Go get the kids. Tell them to come along, then we drive to my place.* But it's turning out to be more complex. For one, Dee is completely spacing out at the notion that Mark is inside the house and will see us trying to gather the kids in the car. She's terrified of what he might try to do if he happens to look out the window when their bus arrives in front of the house. The thought of Mark seeing us outside has Dee trembling and close to tears. I try to assure her things will be okay. When my words fail to comfort her, I give her my cell phone so she can call the house to see if Mark is inside.

"Good, no one's answering," she says.

"See, I told you everything would be just fine," I assure her.

"But you don't understand. Mark keeps his eyes on

the kids like a hawk. It's his way of controlling them and keeping them in line; so they won't think about doing or saying anything against him." Dee's voice is full of anxiety and stress.

"Well, he's in for a rude awakening today, isn't he," I tell her.

"You're way too confident, Lala."

"Jump on the train with me then, Dee. You're getting your kids back, so you might as well get ready."

Dee and I pause briefly and stare at each other. I know we are taking a chance, but I feel good about the prospect of reuniting her with her kids. Going through the red tape was all bullshit to me, anyway. Her kids were being abused and she is living in a shelter because of it. It doesn't sit well with me that Keith can tell me there is nothing that can be done.

Dee says, "Okay, you're right. We can do this." Dee begins mumbling to herself to relax and be calm.

"Since we know he isn't home, we can have the girls go inside, get their things, and then we'll leave," I decide.

"Maybe one of us should go with them?"

"No, let's let them do it. That way, if Mark does come home, we won't be in the house with them. "

"Good," Dee says. "Let's just make sure we tell them if he does come home, to gather their things and we'll pick them up in the morning."

"Exactly," I confirm.

We are both on the lookout for the school bus and Mark.

"Thank you, Lala," Dee says. "Oh…thank you, thank you, thank you," she repeats.

"Dee, we haven't gotten them yet…"

"But still. You're trying to help me. I really appreciate it. You don't know how much I've missed them all."

"I can imagine, Dee. A mother should never be away from her kids."

Dee smiles. "Sean usually gets home a few minutes after the girls. Both of their buses are usually on time."

We sit anxiously for another ten minutes and at the sight of a school bus rolling down the street, Dee opens her door and stands right beside the car.

She watches the bus come to a complete stop. When the bus pulls away, Dee calls out to them. They all meet in the middle of the street hugging and jumping for joy to see one another. I look at my watch and yell out the window for Dee to tell the girls to get going. Dee starts to give them instructions as fast as she can and rushes them all to the driveway, then comes back to the car. No sooner than she gets back to the car, I nod up the street at Sean. He's down the street holding a long stick in his hand swinging it as though it is a baseball bat. Dee jumps out the car and calls his name. When he sees her, he stops as though his feet are in the thickest cement ever made. But he makes sure he calls out to his mother at least ten times before he moves toward her.

"C'mon, boy," Dee yells out to him.

"Mama?"

"Yes, it's me. Come here, hurry up!" Dee instructs.

Sean drops his stick and runs as fast as he can toward his mother. Dee tells him to run in the house and get as many clothes as he can hold and give his sisters the rest. We wait another ten minutes while everyone is inside. All of a sudden, Dee reaches for my horn and starts to have at it.

"I've waited too damn long to be with my kids, Lala. They need to hurry up."

There is nothing I can say because I know she is right. Dee can't take it anymore and she gets out the car and runs in the house. A few minutes later, we are all in the car and I am just about to pull off.

"Wait!" Sean screams.

We all look at him.

"There's my dog! I need to take him with me! There's Joey! I can't leave him!"

Dee looks at me and I look at her. They don't know I am scared as hell of dogs. Especially this big, black, big-headed dog that looks like it would bite your head off with one chomp.

"Okay, go get him," I tell Sean.

And he does. And we are on our way to my place.

Chapter 35

It's close to nine o'clock in the evening before everyone is finally situated. I have more than enough room in the house, and the kids and Dee find spots throughout in which to lay their heads. Dee snuggles up with Sean in the guest room, and I venture out to the store so that I can stock up the refrigerator.

When I finally sit down to relax, I can't fall asleep as easily as everyone else after their loving reunion. I am entirely way too excited about reuniting Dee with her kids that it shoots adrenaline throughout my body. They are all so happy to be together. The girls had their moments, though, which hurt to see. One minute they would be laughing uncontrollably and the next crying their eyes out because of what they had been through with Mark. I don't know where Dee got the strength to talk to them about the situation. But, as I listened, she didn't sugarcoat the truth. She told them what had happened to them is wrong and she assured them it would not go unpunished.

I still hadn't gotten over seeing Keith so unexpectedly. Seeing the dirty rat and finding out what he'd accomplished in the short time we'd been apart, tore at me like a sharp razor's edge. I would've probably been able to deal with seeing him if he hadn't been so nonchalant about our meeting. Ever since meeting Keith, he'd never shown me such disrespect. And not asking me if I was doing okay or how I was making do, made me realize that he didn't give a damn about me anymore and was moving on with his life.

It's about eleven at night when I realize that it is time for me, for once and for all, to move on with my life. Finally get over Keith, start a new chapter. So, like a thief in the night, after I chat with Dee to make sure everyone is okay, I prepare to do what is needed so I can put things behind me. I shower, put on my favorite smell-good, slip on a dress without panties, and I'm out the door.

I call Lorenzo. He is surprised even more so when I let him know that I am five minutes away from his place. To put it lightly I am on a mission—a well-deserved personal assignment that desperately needs to be taken care of without a moment's delay. I have suppressed it long enough. No longer did I feel like letting my life continue to pass me by without at least enjoying myself as a sexual being, even though I no longer had a regular mate to explore with. Plus, the moment has more to do with than just sex. The moment is essential to help me recover from being used. Just glue the door shut a hundred times over to what has happened to me.

When Lorenzo answers the door, his face tells me he knows why I'm here. I don't tell him hello. I walk right past him and find his bedroom like I have been here a hundred times before. He isn't far behind. He brings in a bottle of wine and pours two glasses, then dims the lights. Our clothes are off and we stand directly in front of his bed.

"Look," he says. "I know what this is all about. But don't take offense to me wearing protection, okay."

I had been out the game so long, I almost forgot because Keith and I had been natural since forever.

"Oh, yeah. Not a problem," I tell him.

"And it's not like I don't trust you," he says.

"Oh, it's okay. I prefer it safely, anyway."

"Good, but just so you know. I'm wearing two condoms tonight. It has nothing to do with you. But everything to do with the no-good man who walked away from you."

"You're right, Lorenzo. This is what it's all about."

I tell him to bend down. I take my drink and gently pour it over the top of his head and begin to kiss his chest as it runs down his body. Lorenzo is not to be outdone. He picks me up in one swoop and lays me on his bed. And in a few hours, I had accomplished what I'd come to do.

Chapter 36

I wake up the next morning and my house is in complete verbal chaos. I can't believe how loud three girls, a little boy, and a dog can be. I even get out of my bed to witness the back-and-forth happenings between the siblings and have to drink two cups of coffee before we are off and taking them to school. But it's all good. Dee and her family are happy and full of love. My night with Lorenzo is now a refreshing memory, and I am now motivated and determined to help Dee get her family life in order.

There is a brief point in the morning that I can return calls from Nancy. She has left several messages and by her tone I can tell she really wants to talk. When I call her, she floors me when she asks if I am interested in one of three positions at CMN. I take one quick glance around my house and notice all the new mouths I have committed to take care of. I let her know that I surely am. Then I agree to meet her for lunch.

❖❖❖

I arrive for lunch, and from jump I am impressed with her digs. I only have a brief stay in the reception area. But it is long enough to realize it is furnished with Nani Marquina furniture, and she runs an absolutely no-nonsense operation.

Her receptionist has the most gorgeous smile and warm attitude, making me feel welcome right away. When I walk through the classy wooden, double doors leading into Nancy's office, I am in complete awe. The flooring's immaculately waxed, and I see pictures of different CMN events and coverage. Then there she is sitting behind a huge bare desk with her hands folded and smiling with her well-defined cover girl face.

"C'mon in here," Nancy says. She stands up and the outfit she has on makes the one she wore for dinner look like a thrift-store item. It most definitely has to be straight out of an exclusive boutique in New York City.

I thank her for inviting me. She walks me around her humongous office and there is a essence to every picture hanging on her wall. Nancy then gives me the general scoop on her job duties. After she tells her receptionist to hold all of her calls, she fills me in on the three positions she thinks I would be a perfect match for. One is a producer of a news-related talk show that aired on the weekends. The other is a senior writer for the national news at six. Then there is the executive producer of CMN's *Good Morning Again.*

I am very humble and tell her.

"To say the least, Nancy, I am so very appreciative of what you're doing for me."

"Girl, please, you're qualified for these jobs. I already called up your station and got the goods on you."

"Oh really?"

"Sure did, and the station manager only had kind words for you. And you've been in the industry long enough to bump up a bit, don't you think?"

The smile on my face is so huge I can feel it. "Absolutely."

Nancy opens up a folder and gives me copies of all the job descriptions. We go over them line by line. I am so impressed that she would take the time out of her busy day to help me out in this way. She explains the jobs so well that it makes it very difficult to choose because I am feeling each and every one. So, I ask her if I have to give her a definite answer right away.

"How long do you think you'll need?" Nancy asks.

"Is a week too much time?"

"Not at all, I think it's wise to think things over," she answers. Nancy puts down her folder and then smiles at me wondering. "So, how have things been going?"

"Just fine," I tell her.

"Lala, relax, girl. We are finished talking about the positions for now. This is girl time." She giggles.

"Oh. I'm all for that. In fact, bring out the drinks!"

"You really want something?" Nancy pushes a button. Behind a picture near the corner of her office a small mini bar appears with glasses at the ready.

"Oh, no, no. I was just teasing, but dang, that's nice."

"Well, not me," she says. "I'm on my way home and this has been one hell of a day," she explains. Then she walks over to the bar and tells me she is going to have her favorite—apple martini.

There is a couch and two chairs made by Jasper Morrison near the bar and I sit down on the couch after I give it a compliment. Nancy is amazed that I know so much about furniture. Then I let her know I minored in design in college. I really enjoyed knowing that Nancy is so down-to-earth, especially since a lot of women in Atlanta who have done well in their lives are so guarded and have a hard time of letting anyone in their inner circle. But who can blame them; it's hard for a sista on the come-up.

After insisting her apple martini is to die for, Nancy says, "I was reading *Ebony* the other day and a writer named Joy Bennett Kinnon wrote a perfect article on sistahs and how we treat one another."

"How was it?" I truly wanted to know.

"Fabulous! It was so good that I cut it out and framed it. But the one thing that stuck in my mind was the fact that she said Jada Pinkett Smith told her that 'Everybody needs a Sister Souljah in their life.'"

"That's very nice of her," I let Nancy know.

"Well, I just wanted to tell you that I do, too," she says.

"Really?"

"Absolutely, someone that can keep my head straight and to help me keep that balance. And I really would like you to be that person for me," Nancy says.

"Are you serious?"

"Yes, why not? You're a very intriguing lady with lots of opinions. You are a very good listener and most of all, you're trustworthy. Just a breath of fresh air."

"Yeah, but I ain't no Sister Souljah, though. I heard her speak when she came to Atlanta at sister Fanta's bookstore in Clarkston a few years ago, and she is something fierce."

"I just need you to be yourself."

"No disrespect, Nancy, but wouldn't you rather talk to someone your own age?"

"No." She is flat out with her answer. The way she sounds makes me laugh.

"Why not?"

"Because most of the women my age are for whatever reason so mad at the world right now."

"Really?"

"You wouldn't believe it. I mean I love my friends, but when I call them, it's the same story. They are either fed up with their grown-ass children, torn up from their neglecting-ass husbands, or too tired and out of shape to get out the house and live a little bit," she says.

"Oh, stop it…"

"I'm serious. You'll keep that fire in me that I need. With you to talk to, I'll see myself in you and share your motivation. And there's no doubt you won't just tell me what you think I want to hear. You understand what I'm saying?"

"Yes, I do, Nancy."

"Plus, you know my husband. And God knows, I need someone to help me with understanding him."

I am hesitant before I speak. "Did Sydney tell you that I spoke with him?"

Nancy is just about finished with her drink and looks down in her glass before answering. "Yes, he did. He told me that he saw you."

"But did he tell you what I said to him?"

"No. But I could tell it was something."

"You're right. I told him that you were thinking about getting a divorce. I let him know that he better hurry up and realize what was going on with himself before he lost the best thing he ever had."

Nancy smiles.

"And I mean that, Nancy."

"Well, thank you, Lala."

"You're welcome."

"But, I'm not getting a divorce now," Nancy blurts out.

"No…?"

"No. I made a commitment and I have to stand by it."

I am relieved that she has come to this conclusion. "Well, just keep working on him. I'm sure he'll come around," I tell her.

She smiles. "I'm sure he will.

Nancy stands up and pours another drink. "Would you like one, Lala?"

I stand up, too. "Sure, why not?" Then we toast to friendship.

Chapter 37

That same day I'm in the kitchen showing Dee the job descriptions of the positions I have to choose from. I'm trying to get my head right because I have planned to see Lorenzo again later. I am about halfway through reading to Dee the prospects of the position as a producer when I realize something is wrong. I ask her if she is okay.

Her tone is painful, similar to what I remember at the shelter. "A man came over while you were gone," she says.

"A man, what man?"

"Said his name was Keith?"

"Shit. Keith? That's my ex. What did he want?"

"He knocked. I answered and he said he wanted to talk to you."

"What else did he say?"

"He wanted to know where you were. I told him that you weren't here and then he wanted to know who I was."

"He asked you that?"

Dee nods her head. "I told him my name and it was like a light went off in his head."

"Dee, Keith is my ex. He's the lawyer that works for the center that told us that they wouldn't help us with Mark."

"Well, I'm sure he knows who I am. He even saw the girls and asked if we lived here."

I am quick. "What'd you say?"

"Told him we were just visiting."

"Good. Good." I start to think about what Keith could have wanted. We had no unfinished business. I put my job descriptions down and decided to look at them later.

"Look, don't answer the door while I'm gone tonight, okay? If he comes back here, you call me on my cell."

Before I leave, I tell Dee not to worry, then order pizza for the gang.

For some reason Lorenzo wants to see Spike Lee's film *She Hate Me*. I find out later it's only because he hasn't seen it yet and can never get it on DVD. At first I don't want to go. For some reason, I just want him to take me back to his bedroom again and fuck me. I am still in my "letting go and move forward" mode. But after he reads to me the description of the movie, I begin to think it just might be a good idea to see what Mr. Lee's film is all about.

We drive out to an old, cheesy, one-dollar theater with three screens and to my surprise, it is jam-packed.

But when we walk into our movie, we have our choice of seats and then some. It trips me out how Lorenzo counts every single row of seats in the theater, then grabs me by the hand and sits in the middle row of the theater. I look at him through the darkness like he is crazy, and he tells me that we are sitting in the best seats in the house. Not too close. Not too far away but right in the middle where we can enjoy the surround sound and picture. *Okay…*While we wait for the movie to come on, it is like Lorenzo has forgotten about the night of sex we shared. He doesn't mention it once. I kind of liked that, but I couldn't wait to bring up the subject, anyway.

"So, you get enough the other night?"

He looks over at me. "Enough?"

"Yeah, enough. Did you get enough?"

"I don't know what you talkin' 'bout," he says.

"Don't play. You know what I'm talking about."

"No, really I don't."

I am really pushing my new attitude and his game playing makes me play a game of my own. So, I place my hand where I think Lorenzo's manhood is and I be damned if he isn't hard as a rock. "Oh, you don't know what I'm talking 'bout, hunh?"

He tries to move away a bit.

"Sure don't," he answers.

"Well, your Johnson says different," I tell him.

Lorenzo finally smiles and kisses me on the neck. "No,

I didn't get enough. And you keep on, I'm going to get some right here."

"Oh really now?"

"Really."

I swear, it is so hard making it through the movie thinking about what is coming next. To top it off, it is a long movie and I enjoy it, but I want to go back to Lorenzo's to feel some of that hard in his pants.

We are in the car. Quiet. Both more than likely thinking of what we want to do to each other. I know I am. I don't know why I say anything but I feel that I can at the time.

"Look, I have something to tell you," I say to him.

"Sure, what is it?"

"After I left our so-called counsel for the center the other day, I went down to the shelter and picked up Sean's mom."

"Really? Where'd you two go—lunch or something?"

"No. To pick up her kids at her house."

Lorenzo starts laughing. "Yeah, right. Good one."

"I'm serious…"

I feel the car slow down a bit. "Lala, tell me you're not serious?"

"Look. I did it because…I did it because I didn't like Keith telling me that I couldn't do something. More than that, Dee needs to be with her kids."

"Lala, how could you do something like that?"

"Hey, I just did. They are fine and happy now."

"Do you know what type of trouble the center can get into?"

"Trouble? Why would the center get into trouble?"

"Because you're attached to it and it brings up all types of ethical questions of who you're working on behalf of."

"Don't even sweat it because I'm working on my own behalf."

Lorenzo makes a left-hand turn into his driveway, then looks at me before he stops. "Fuck it. I'm much too horny to think about this now." Then he grabs me and puts his lips on mine.

I recall an episode of *Sex in the City* where one of the characters said it was impossible to have good sex with a man the first few times. I don't know who the hell those ladies had been doing it with, but Lorenzo is the real deal and to tell the truth, he has my whole body on fire. After our session, though, Lorenzo looks down and realizes that the condom has broken.

Chapter 38

I am on my way home from Lorenzo's. I have the radio on and listening to "Quiet Storm." The DJ is playing a sizzling, old school Lillo Thomas hit that I remember vividly because Keith and I once had a picnic and he played it on his boom box. But while the song is playing, this time all I can do is think about how quickly my life has changed and how difficult it really is getting back into the game as a single woman. It takes guts, courage, and intestinal fortitude to overcome the challenge. And that's when I begin to wonder what happens to women who never can bounce back from a bad experience with a man. There is so much pressure, competition, if they want to admit it or not, and lies to waddle through to even begin starting anew.

I don't know why but I am almost in tears. I have a good time with Lorenzo. But "time" is the key word, and the time spent was actually a moment. The sex. I knew that after a while, like it always does, would fade and both parties would want more—maybe nothing more and call it a day. The newness of being with someone else, learning their story and view of life is interesting, but having a condom burst while he is still up inside me is not something that I could regularly get used to or ever wanted to happen. The notion of it happening makes my conscience speak to me. It reminds me that I never had to worry about this kind of shit with Keith. Matter of fact, it told me that when *he* came inside me, I felt so good.

Lillo's song *I Wanna Make Love To You* is fading as the DJ's voice begins taking over the airwaves. I turn on my blinker and then onto my street. I almost lose it when I see at least four police cars in front of my house with lights blaring uncontrollably. The cars are parked so tactically that I have to park on my lawn. I start to run into the house, and I hear my name being called over Joey's constant bark inside. It is Mark. He appears through the flashing lights and darkness growling like he is King Kong's brother or something. I stop and wait for him to approach me.

"The next time you want to have a sleepover, call me first," he snarls.

I look at him, then over to my house. "What the hell is going on? What are the police doing in my house?"

"The party's over," he says. "My kids are coming home with me and you are lucky if I don't decide to press kidnapping charges on your ass."

"Kidnapping? What are you…"

"Look, I said what I needed to say to you. Look at these kids coming out of your house. This definitely couldn't be good for them."

I tried to focus my eyes through the darkness and flashing lights. The girls all have been awakened and have blankets over their bodies, as they are being escorted by a policewoman. When they walk over close to us, the girls are dazed and confused because it is close to two in the morning. I try to reach out to them but Mark steps in and gives them all a kiss on the forehead as they file by. I am about to vomit when he tells them he loves them and has missed them so very much. I want so very badly to smack his face. I want to hit him as hard as I can for making the kids' lives so very difficult. But I dismiss the thought when I overhear an officer say they can't find Sean. I watch the girls sit down in the back of Mark's car, and I give him one last good stare and go in the house to see about Sean and Dee.

I can see through the door that there are signs of some type of struggle. One of my chairs is lying on the floor and the throw rugs on my hardwood floors are crumpled and out of place. I am terrified when I see a officer pull his pistol out and aim it right at the dog who seems like he is ready to attack at any minute. One of the officers at the front door wants to know my name. When I tell him and let him know he is standing in my house, he backs off. I look over in my TV room and there is Dee holding Sean as tight as she can in my recliner, rocking back and forth as another female officer stands with outstretched arms ready to take Sean outside.

"Dee?"

Dee lifts her face from Sean's embrace. One look at her

and I almost start to cry myself. Dee is in another world. She and Sean have been crying and she is so surprised at what is going on that she can barely talk to me.

"They're not taking my child, Lala."

The female officer standing over Dee has a very bad attitude. Her tone is nasal and nasty. "Ma'am, I'm telling you for the last time. Give me the boy."

"Hold on a second," I tell her.

"Excuse me?" the officer pops off.

"You heard me. That's her son. Not yours."

"And who are you?"

"I live here, if it matters to you."

"Well, ma'am, she needs to either let the child go or walk with us out the house, so we can take him where he belongs."

"He belongs here, with me," Dee says as strong as she can under the circumstances. "All of my children belong with me," she tells the officer.

"Like I told you, ma'am, you don't have custody of these children. So they have to go with who has custody," she says over the sound of the barking dog.

"And I keep asking you are you sure he has full custody?"

"According to the paperwork we've seen, ma'am, yes, he does."

I can't believe what I am hearing and I interrupt. "How does he have full custody? She adopted these children and that little boy is her flesh and blood."

"Ma'am, he told us that after she left he went downtown, filed the necessary paperwork, and was granted full legal custody of them all."

I look down at Dee holding Sean and wish like hell there is something I can do. "Dee, you're going to have to let him go," I tell her but I'm frustrated.

"But I can't let them go back there, Lala."

Sean scoots up inside his mother's grasp like he wants to go back into her womb.

"I know, but he has custody. He has the right, according to the law. Let them go, but be certain I will make sure you get them back."

"How, by using the lawyer who more than likely called and told them where they were? You think your ex wants my case, Lala? Men ain't shit!" Dee screams.

In an instant there is complete silence when the dog stops barking and falls hard on the floor to his side. Everyone looks at a policeman who walks over to the now limp dog.

He says, "It's only a tranquilizer. He will be back up in a few hours."

The female officer tells Dee that Sean has to go one more time but Dee doesn't release Sean. A male officer walks over and pries her arms from around him. Sean painfully screams to be with his mother. The officer walks out the door with Sean and Dee gets up from the chair.

"I'm going home, Lala," she says.

"What?"

"I have to go. They don't know what this man will do to them, and I will not let it happen again," she says.

I try to talk to Dee, but she runs out the house to be with her kids, and I can't say I blame her one bit.

Chapter 39

Now this is where I am with mine.

If Keith thought he could cheat on me, make a baby, move out, then in with the mother of his child, call the police about matters that really didn't concern him, he must have been crazy!

At this point, Keith doesn't know it, but I have already heard about the new house he has moved into with Adria. It only takes me one phone call to the television station to find out where he and Adria are staying. It is funny because the person I receive the information from is working the night shift and Adria is on days. But she has been running her mouth about how nice their new place is, putting her business on blast, and everyone is starting to get tired of all her perceived goodness.

While driving I can feel that Keith and the entire situation is making me into someone I really don't want to be. I don't care that it's in the wee hours of the morning when I ring their doorbell.

Keith opens the door trying to act all sleepy and shit.

"Lala? What the fuck?"

"Don't you 'what the fuck' me," I scream.

"Excuse me?"

"Please, don't you mock me. Do you wanna do this out here or are you going to let me in?"

Keith looks around outside and up toward his neighbors' windows. I can tell he is thinking, *let me get this bitch inside before the tenant association hears about this.* Keith ushers me in with his hand and his head down. I walk straight into his place and don't give one good damn that I accidentally step on his bare foot with my hard-ass shoes.

"Lala, I think you need to calm down."

"What?"

"Calm down. You're knocking on my door. Stepping on my feet. What the hell is wrong with you? Are you just now hitting a boiling point over me and Adria or something because if you are, this is not the time. I already told you that I was sorry, but the shit's over."

I am dumbfounded by his nerve. "This has nothing to do with Adria and your child," I let him know.

"No?"

"No," I repeat again.

"Then what?"

"And you have the nerve to stand there like you haven't done anything, Keith. Just like you stood in my face for all those years and you were fucking Adria."

"What are you talking about?"

I am still for a moment with a willing smile on my face. Just taking all his shit in. I can't believe how well he thinks he is hiding his call to the police. "Let me ask you something? Do your parents ever regret letting you be born? I mean, do you really think I'm incapable of realizing what you've done? You have no shame, do you?"

"Lala, I really wish I knew what you were talking about. Now look, I have a very busy day and either you tell me what you're talking about or leave."

Adria peeks around the corner. She is wearing a housecoat and rubbing her eyes.

"Keith, what's going on?" She looks me up and down without speaking.

"Oh, you two deserve each other," I let them know.

"Keith, what is she talking about?"

"Don't worry about it. I'm going to take care of it, okay?"

"Well, if she wakes the baby, there's going to be a problem."

"Listen, there's already a problem. Keith, you didn't have to tell the police those kids and their mother were staying with me. What you did was put those girls back into a situation they don't deserve."

"What the hell are you talking about? I haven't called the police on anybody for anything."

"Well, I'm about to," Adria decides. "Coming up in my house yelling and screaming like you don't have any damn sense." Adria walks away.

"Go 'head! Call them, you skank bitch!"

"Lala, I came over your house to tell you that I was sorry for the way I acted in the office the other day, and the lady Dee, that's her name, answers the door. But I think you better leave now," Keith says. "I'm serious. You don't need to be going to jail."

I walk right past Keith after I call him a liar and tell him to go to hell.

Chapter 40

I am surprised at the knock on my door the next day. I have no clue as to who it could be, because the police and the Animal Control Agency just left twenty minutes prior to take Sean his dog.

I look out the peephole, and there is Nancy standing erect, holding a stunning Coach bag and wearing a fancy red suit that is highlighted nicely with cream pearls. I can vaguely see her black Town Car and driver sitting behind her on the street. I open the door and say hello.

"Now, you look like you could use a good hot lunch," she says. "Are you ready to go?"

"Damn. Lunch—I completely forgot, Nancy." We stand for a moment wondering what to do next. Having lunch with Nancy might have been on my agenda, but my mind is not on lunch at all. I shake off my slight daze.

"Look, I have some croissants, turkey, and all the dressings that we can do right here."

"Sounds good to me," Nancy agrees.

We go back into my kitchen and I am so happy Nancy

doesn't ask me why my place is such a mess. It looks pretty much the same way as the night before when the police came over, guns blazing, for the kids. I did manage to pick up the chairs that had been knocked down. But my place still isn't as sharp as I usually keep it.

I prepare the food. Croissants with turkey, tomatoes, and lettuce and a nice bowl of tomato soup.

"You know? This is better than going out," Nancy assures. "Everything's fresh. There's no distractions. You seem a bit uneasy, though."

"Rough night."

"Sometimes that can be a good thing. Just matters what category you're talking about."

"Oh, it's in the worst possible way. Enough to totally throw a person off track."

"Well, don't worry and join the club."

"You, too?"

Nancy nods in agreement and takes a bite of her sandwich.

"But you hide yours so well," I let her know.

"If you have been down and out as long as I have, it's easy to do. So, wanna talk about it?"

"No, not really. But when I do, I promise I will," I tell her.

"I've just about come to the conclusion that what I'm going through is my own damn fault."

"Nancy, you can't blame yourself. It takes two."

"But if I would have thought about what Sydney was

asking me before I just arbitrarily jumped in head first, more than likely I would have told him to take his open relationship bullshit and drop it in the lake."

I am sincere when I say to her, "Nancy, knowing what I do about Sydney, I don't think he's done anything that would compromise you two."

"But the fact remains, what would make him want to do this at all?"

"What makes men do half the things they do?"

"You asked him, didn't you?"

"I did, but it wasn't like an answer that you could just take and understand where he was coming from. The only thing it really made me feel was that I was not good enough for him anymore."

"I doubt that very seriously, Nancy."

"Well, it's all too confusing for me and what it has come down to, is that I still have a man that wants to be with me as he has done for years, or he does not want to be at all."

At the moment I can't answer for Sydney. I want to, in order to keep Nancy from crying, but it isn't my place. Nancy wipes a tear from her eye right before it falls down her cheek. She is holding onto more pain than she initially admits. From the few times I have sat down to chat with her, I cannot understand why Sydney has come to the conclusion he has. But then again he is a man, so I shouldn't expect to understand. The only thing that I can even try to piece together is that after

Sydney closed up his restaurant, he became bitter and felt like a failure and began to push Nancy away. But Nancy dismisses my notion after she tells me that it was Sydney's plan all along after he made enough money from the restaurant to close it down.

Nancy and I have a good lunch, all things considered. I tell her I am leaning toward the producer position, and she is all smiles and tells me she can't wait until I start.

After lunch I finally get a chance to sleep uninterrupted. But the bad thing about my rest is that I have a dream about the girls being raped throughout the day and Dee being forced to watch as they cry out for help.

I wake up when the phone rings. It freaks me out because it's Dee. It's so good to hear her voice but hard to shake the dream.

"How are the kids?" I just have to know.

"I don't know," she says.

I rush to say, "What do you mean?"

"Haven't really gotten a chance to talk to them yet. Mark has been watching me like I'm some type of criminal or something."

"Are you home now?"

"No. At the grocery store. On the pay phone. I just wanted to let you know that we were all right and thanks for trying."

"Dee, I'm sorry Keith's sorry ass did that to you and the kids."

"Don't worry about it, Lala. We all know that it wasn't your fault."

"So, what are you going to do now?"

I can tell Dee is thinking on the other end.

"Well, I think I gotta make this work here, Lala."

"Dee…"

"No, hear me out. If I stay, I think it will be okay this time."

"Why would you think that? Mark is a fuckin' moron who needs to be put in jail."

"I know it, and you know it, Lala."

"But now, see he doesn't know what I've told you about what he's been doing. He's wondering and he's scared. If I can keep him this way, he'll stop his shit and we'll be able to move on, at least until I can get my own place."

"No, Dee, that's just too big of a risk to take."

"You should see him, Lala. He's walking on eggshells. I thought he would get us here and it would start all over again."

"But you've only been there one night."

"It's just a feeling I have, that's all."

"How is Sean? Is he okay?"

"Yes, he just wants to be with me. Lala, he's happy when I'm around so I'm going to stay here without a ripple of trouble. I think that's the best way to do this."

"Dee, are you sure?"

"I am."

"Do me a favor, Dee."

"Sure, anything, Lala, you've been so nice to us."

"Make sure Sean continues to go to the center, okay? That way, I'll be able to see him."

"You've really fallen for my boy, haven't you?"

"He's amazing…"

"He sure is," Dee affirms. "Oh, before I forget. What's the guy you're seeing at the center's name again?"

"You mean, Lorenzo?"

"Yeah, that's him," Dee says.

"What about him?"

"I heard a message that he left on the answering machine."

"A message? What message?"

"It was for Mark. He asked Mark to call him."

"When was this, Dee?"

"It had to be before we moved back in because our phone hasn't rung since," Dee figures.

Chapter 41

Thirty minutes after talking to Dee, I make my way over to Lorenzo's.

"Dee tells me you called Mark?"

"Dee tell you that?"

"Yeah, told me you left a message for Mark to call you?"

"Oh yeah, that's right, I did."

"May I ask about what?"

"I really can't, Lala. It's like confidential."

"Confidential. What? The man that molests his daughters has a confidentiality clause in your estimation?"

"Look, Lala, I think it's time for you to know something," he says. I am close to asking him what it is, during his extended pause. "I'm the one who told Mark where his family was. I told him they were all living with you."

"You told him? Why would you tell him that?"

There is another pause. "Because he needed to know. Plus, Mark and I have been seeing each other going on three years now."

I heard what Lorenzo said. *Seeing each other?* But it

doesn't register and leaves me confused. Then quickly, just like it happened when I found out that Keith was the father of Adria's child, I begin to get super hot all over my body as though I've been set ablaze. "Seeing him?"

"Yes, we've been on the DL tip, Lala. It's time you knew."

"The DL? So, that's when two stupid-ass men sleep together, right?" I can't believe Lorenzo's arrogance.

"I wouldn't call them 'stupid.'" He chuckles.

"So, I'm right then?"

"Yes, Lala, you're right. We were together for about three years, then broke it off recently."

I try to laugh it off. "Lorenzo, this better be a joke."

"No, I think it's time that you knew," he says.

After hearing his words, I have never shouted so loud in my life. "*I should've known before you ever put your nasty hands on me!*"

"Wait, so, now all of a sudden, I'm nasty?"

"Nigga, I can't believe what's coming out of your mouth! Yes, you're nasty! You sleep with men. What the hell would make you want to do that, then try and deal with me?"

I have been transformed into a madwoman in a second's notice. I hate feeling this way but there is no other option for me. Lorenzo has totally betrayed my trust. He could have told me he was married; or had five children by five different women; even an ex-con, who served twenty years for murder and I wouldn't have been as mad as I am at him. There are just way too many things rushing through my mind as I stand looking at this man who I have slept with. I hate that he is looking back at me like it was just another day at the office and doesn't mean a damn thing.

"Oh my God, you came in me, Lorenzo!"

"If you remember, the condom broke," he says.

"I don't give a damn what happened. You did."

"So, what are you saying?"

"I want to know if you've ever taken an AIDS test!"

"AIDS test? For what?"

I want to scream. "Since you fuck men. Or do you get fucked?"

He laughs me off.

"I want to know if you have the virus."

"Lala, you're making too much out of this. No, I don't have any virus."

"How in the fuck do you know, if you've never been tested?"

"Do I look sick to you?"

"Do not hit me up with those childish-ass answers. It doesn't matter what you look like. I need to know what a test says," I tell him.

"Well, the answer to your question is, I've never taken one."

I can't even believe I am having this conversation. "And you've been gay...how long?"

"Bitch, I'm not gay," he says. "So, watch your mouth."

"Not gay?"

"No, I'm not. I'm on the *DL*," he says.

"You motherfuckers get on my nerves with this shit! If you sleep with men, you're gay, you stupid bastard."

"Lala, you're entitled to your opinion. I'm not gay. I have sex with men when I can't with a woman. That's it, I just like to get mine."

"Well, that's nasty. And your black ass is going to take an AIDS test!"

"No, I'm not."

"Oh, nigga, yes, you are."

"I think you better leave, Lala."

"Leave?"

"That's right."

"After dumping this shit on me, you tellin' me to leave?"

"Yes, you have to go. I can see you don't understand this lifestyle and there's nothing else to talk about."

"You're right, I don't. But I tell you what…"

"What's that?"

"You will be taking that AIDS test, Mr. Lifestyle. Trust me, you will."

Chapter 42

There is a continuous blaring echo in my brain. *Lorenzo is on the DL. Lorenzo is on the DL…*I am still parked in his driveway hyperventilating and trying to suppress all the shit going through my mind telling me what I should do. I can't lie. I want to hurt him. Make his head spin as fast; faster than mine. The only reason I haven't pulled out of his driveway is because my hands are shaking too badly to drive. I struggle to get my cell out of my purse. I drop it on the floor twice before I am able to call.

"Sydney?"

"Lala? You okay?

"No…"

"What's wrong…why are you crying?"

"Sydney, I need to see you. Where are you, at the bar?"

"Yes, are you hurt?"

"Yes, I mean, no, not physically. I hope."

"You hope? Either you are or you aren't."

"That's what I always thought, Sydney, until tonight. I'll be there as soon as I can."

Sydney doesn't understand before we hang up and neither do I. I've never been too shallow to think homosexuality didn't exist. But I never had to really worry about it. But I wasn't in a so-called monogamous relationship anymore. I was out in it—a pond of fuckin' who done it and what for. I'd been too naive to freakin' realize that I could be deceived and made to believe that I was in a sexual relationship with a man who was *straight*.

Right then I want retribution. I want to sue; do something but there is no law that says a man has to tell a woman when he's sleeping with both sexes. In my mind Lorenzo is trash. There is absolutely nothing he can tell me that will make what I am feeling right. The thought of him having sex with another man, makes me pull over three times and vomit on my way to see Sydney. Just thinking of this man possibly placing his mouth on Mark and those two touching and sharing intimate moments is enough to make me want to let go of the steering wheel and crash my car. When I finally get to the bar, I throw myself into a seat and ask Sydney to order me whatever he is drinking.

"No, no, baby girl, you don't want this," he explains.

"Yes, I do," I tell him.

"This drink is not for ladies," he assures me.

"Fuck it. The rules are changing tonight," I insist.

Sydney points over to the bar and raises two fingers after motioning to his glass. "Lala, what is going on with you?"

"Let me get my drink first, Sydney."

"Little lady, your hands are shaking."

"Sydney, please...," I rant.

Sydney sits back and lights a cigar. Nice and cool.

"Can I have one of those, too?"

"You want one of these?"

"Sydney, please, give me one, gotdamn it."

Sydney reaches into his suit jacket, pulls another out, and hands it to me. I snatch it from his hand and his lighter is not far behind. I puff and puff, as I have watched him do so many times, to get it started.

Sydney says, "Gotdamn, Lala, you are in some fuckin' kind of good mood tonight."

The drinks come and I look down at mine. Before the bartender has walked away from our table, I have already shoved it down.

Sydney looks up. "Whoa....whoa... You trying to kill yourself? You don't drink top-shelf Scotch like that, mama..."

I look at the bartender whose eyes are wondrous now and ask for another.

"Aight. Lala. Tell me what the fuck is going on," Sydney says.

"You want to know?"

"You came here to tell me, didn't you?"

I puff on the irritating cigar again and realize it is better to smell than actually taste, so I put it down in the ashtray in front of Sydney. "Lorenzo is gay."

Sydney's eyes tighten, then he takes his glass and throws back his drink faster than I did mine. "Say what?"

"He's gay. Take it like I tell you, then accept it, because that's how it was explained to me."

"Accept it? Hold on, you're moving too fast."

"This shit hurts too much to talk about, Sydney."

"Then take your time." Sydney looks at the bartender and he is busy so he pulls a shorty of Scotch out his suit jacket and pours it in our glasses.

"Fuck it. Drink it. But slow down and tell me."

I take another sip and my head is starting to spin. "What the hell am I drinking?"

"I told you, Scotch. Now, what's the matter?"

"Sydney. I was over Lorenzo's and he told me he was on the *DL*."

Sydney squints his eyes, then swipes his face and his words are slow and complete. "He-told-you-that?"

"Sure did. Tonight," I say back.

"What the…I don't understand?"

"You? I don't, either. We were talking and all of a sudden, he tells me that he is the one who called the police and told them Dee and her kids were staying with me."

"Why would he do that?"

"Because he's fucking her husband, Mark," I let him know.

Sydney stands up and tells the bartender to bring the bottle. "You know I have a lot to say about a lot of things," he says.

"But this ain't one of them, is it?"

Sydney shakes his head no. "I've never understood it, Lala. I'm from the old school where niggas grew up wanting to have the finest lady around. Did whatever we could to get her. Never thought about sleeping with no damn man."

"I know, Sydney. I mean this asshole acts like it's nothing but a thang, like it was just an everyday occurrence to tell me they were sleeping together."

"Damn it," Sydney echoes.

"When I think about all the shit going around."

Sydney looks at me quickly as he puffs away.

"I'm talking about diseases and shit. Do you know I asked him if he ever had an AIDS test and he told me no?"

"That's what he said?"

"And told me he wasn't taking one, either."

"What kind of man would sleep with another man and a woman, not tell her, and then not take the test?"

"Shit. Lorenzo's stupid ass."

I could see fire burning in Sydney's eyes. "You want him to take it?"

"Hell yes! I'm not trying to die out here over some bullshit."

Sydney takes his phone out his suit jacket and calls someone to pick him up.

"Where are you going?"

"To see this Lorenzo cock sucker—he don't know it yet, but he's about to take an AIDS test."

Chapter 43

Sydney follows me home with a car full of older men, all wearing hats and dark suits. I ask him what he is going to do and he tells me once again it's best if I don't know. He is mad and again I enjoy someone actually caring for me in this type of way. Seeing a man mad about what someone has done to me is a rush at the time, even though I am pissed, too. I have missed that by not knowing my father, but Sydney takes my welfare personal and tells me so.

There is no use trying to go to sleep. I just can't. Plus, my phone is ringing all through the night, seems like every twenty to twenty-five minutes. When I answer, all I can hear is a dial tone. I begin to dread even going to bed. My initial thought is that the liquor I huffed down is going to knock me out. But I look over at the clock and it is five in the morning. Sydney hasn't called me yet and I am afraid to call him. I try to keep my mind from what is going on but I start to wander. Then all of a sudden I start thinking about Dee and the girls because they could be in danger, too. *The nerve of two men who are supposed to be protectors of women lying up together with no shame.* It's nasty, creepy, disrespectful on all levels—just no way to justify it in my mind.

I begin to wish Adria and Keith never went behind my back. Maybe Keith and I would be in the kitchen again, eating breakfast without these worries. I didn't like being a part of a single-female clique who wanted men in our lives but lived with the possibility of losing our lives with one slip-up which I was hoping I hadn't made.

I was pretty sure Dee didn't know anything about Mark being on the DL. How do they come up with these labels, anyway? To me, a man who sleeps with another man is a PUNK, especially when he endangers another person's life. I remember Dee telling me that Mark usually leaves the house around eight-thirty in the morning so I wait until nine to call her.

We only exchange pleasantries before I tell her what is on my mind.

"What do you mean, the *DL*?" she wants to know.

"You know. They have been together for almost three years—*sexually*."

She kind of laughs back into the phone. "Lala, I know you want me and the kids out of here but we are going to be okay, I promise."

My phone rings and I ask Dee to hold, but no one answers on the other end, so I click back over.

"No, Dee, you don't understand. Lorenzo told me himself just last night. He said that he and Mark were in a relationship."

Dee is quiet.

"I couldn't believe it myself. I still don't want to."

"Lala, I don't think Mark would do that." Dee's voice has tightened a bit.

"I don't mean to sound drastic, but did you ever think of him molesting the girls?"

"But on the down-low. Mark? No...he loves women too much for that."

"I wouldn't tell you if it wasn't true, Dee. Have you ever asked him how he knows Lorenzo?"

"No, because the only time I ever really heard of him was when I heard his message."

"Well, Lorenzo told me himself. Told me as though it was no big deal to him. I wanted to smack his face like you wouldn't believe. The nerve of him putting my life in jeopardy like it means nothing, and yours and the girls' as well."

Again, my phone chimes in. I ask Dee to hold again, but there is no answer and I decide not to click over if it happens again.

"Sorry, I'm back, Dee."

"I just want to know, if all this is true, how are we in..."

"Dee..."

"Oh, my goodness. Are you saying AIDS?"

"Well, at least the virus; they put us all at risk and we need to get tested."

"I mean how? How would they have known each other?"

"I wondered the same thing but I remember seeing Eastern Michigan diplomas. When I asked Lorenzo about it when I first met him, he told me he didn't know Mark. But come to find out, Lorenzo is the one who called Mark and told him you and the kids were staying at my place."

"He told you that?"

"Sure did, like he was proud," I tell her.

I heard Dee sniffle on the other end of the phone. "Dee, don't worry. We are going to have to be strong through this together."

"How do you tell girls so young that we have to get AIDS tests because their father molested them and is on the *DL*?"

"I know, it's not going to be easy, but Dee, you have to do it."

"Did Lorenzo tell you he had the disease, Lala?"

"No."

Dee sighs. "Well, there's nothing to worry about then. I mean, if he doesn't…"

"No, there's need for concern, Dee," I let her know.

"What?"

"He's never had a test himself."

Chapter 44

With everything going on, I come very close to calling Nancy on my first day of work and postponing the start of my new job for a week. She would have definitely wanted a reason and I am not nearly ready to divulge any circumstances. So I nix the idea. Plus, I have yet to fill out any type of benefits that my job offers. I want to make sure I have full coverage just in case I have anything to worry about with Lorenzo.

Nancy meets me at my office and introduces me to everyone who possibly matters and is connected to developing the show. I take the introductions by Nancy as a *don't mess with my girl* type of meet-and-greet, and I'm sure the others do, too. She is cordial but lets them all know that I'm a special hire and anything I need is to be given. I am surprised at how many men are going to be working on the show as well. There is absolutely no attraction to any of them, but for some reason, I wonder continuously if they all are on the *DL* while we sit and talk about the possibilities of our show.

My day goes on forever. After the walk with Nancy, I go back to her office to fill out my benefits package where I take out the maximum on all the insurance and leave Sean as my beneficiary. There is no one else in my life that I feel would benefit more from it. While I am looking at the package, I go back in time where for the past eight years, Keith has been my beneficiary. Then I wonder if I was *his* even though he said that I was. I feel myself becoming so distrusting by Keith's and Lorenzo's actions, there's no reason for such nonsense.

Late in the afternoon, Nancy once again taps on my door. She is smiling.

"First days are chaotic, aren't they?"

I smile at her. "I can't even lie…they are in the most way. I'm worn out."

"It's always good to get the first day out of the way. Everyone is very eager to start working with you, Lala."

"Well, I welcome the change of scenery and can't wait to get cracking on the show."

Nancy sits down and crosses her legs in a chair across from my desk. I can't help but admire her Jimmy Choo shoes. "So, Sydney tells me you stopped by the club last night?"

I am not shocked that Nancy asks the question, but her tone is sort of investigating. I have a few extra seconds to gather my thoughts because she notices that my telephone on my desk has not been changed out to the newer models. She speaks of making a mental note to get it taken care of. I damn sure didn't want to tell her the real reason I stopped by the club because I am scared to death about it, not to mention embarrassed. I'm also not sure what exactly happened when Sydney went to see Lorenzo, and I don't want to be identified by anyone that I even knew he and his friends had paid him a visit.

"Yeah, I needed to get away so I stopped by," I tell her.

Nancy lowers her voice a bit. "You know, Sydney came home last night later than usual. What a man his age does out in the streets so late is beyond me…"

"Have you ever hung out with him?"

"No, too afraid of what I might find out."

"Afraid? But that's your husband."

"I used to go to his restaurant all the time, but some of the people that started to hang out on a regular basis scared me."

There is an eccentric pause between us. When I look up from my desk at Nancy, she has somewhat of a wondering glow.

"You know we have separate places, right?"

"Yes, he told me."

"But last night he told me he was staying with me. I waited up for Sydney as long as I could. I thought a romantic evening would be fun. But when he didn't show up at his regular time, I gave him a call and he told me not to wait up because he needed to do something."

"So, you guys haven't talked yet?"

"It's just so depressing. He continues to reject my requests that we talk about our relationship."

"I just don't get it. I've always got the feeling that Sydney was an open-minded man who didn't mind sharing his feelings."

Nancy looks around. "I told my psychiatrist the same thing."

I inch up closer to my desk and lower my voice. "You're seeing someone about this?"

"I had to do something, Lala. Sydney has been in my life forever. We've been hand in glove since I first met him, but I just don't feel we are as close as we once were."

"I've always wondered about a professional to talk to," I tell her.

"I admit, I was a bit apprehensive about going to talk to someone. But the distance I feel between me and Sydney is something new and I don't like it. I've never had to deal with it before because he's always been so close to me."

Nancy giggles. "At times, too close," she remembers.

"And that's what you want from him now? You want him to be there for you?"

"He's always been there for me. I just want to feel the closeness that we once had."

I don't know what to say to Nancy. I do think that she is lucky to have a man. In my eyes she is very fortunate to have a solid man who at least tells her the truth about how he is feeling, at least up to this point. I wonder, as I listen, if Sydney's honesty about wanting more space sparked the concern she had about their relationship. Nancy told me all about the doctor she'd been seeing.

He was a brother who she thought had a very good ear—especially when it came to middle-aged men and how they felt when they reached a certain point in their lives. I wasn't happy to hear though that he told Nancy most marriages that had seemingly sustained the test of many years falter when the man seems to be looking to place more distance between his partner.

Chapter 45

I am so tired after work. It is just shy of six o'clock. I'm already on my couch and prepared to shut my eyes but the doorbell rings. I look through the peephole and it's Dee. I open the door and by the look of her downcast appearance she is going through something very pressing. I'm almost afraid to ask her what is wrong, but I do anyway.

"I took the girls to get tested."

I feel my heart skip a beat. This time I really am afraid to say anything.

"They're scared out of their minds, Lala. I had to get away to clear my head."

"When did you take them?"

"This morning. First, I had to explain what was going on. Then after they all finished crying, they all decided that they wanted to know."

"When will you know?"

"They told me to call back this evening to get our results."

"Have you called yet?"

Dee shakes her head no. "I'm terrified, Lala. I can't help but wonder what I'll do if everything isn't okay."

I know exactly how Dee feels. I have been trying to suppress the anxiety of waiting to hear from Sydney about Lorenzo most of the day.

About fifteen minutes pass and Dee is sitting beside me on the couch crying because the stress is beginning to beat on her.

All of a sudden she shouts, "These fuckin' men!"

"Damn bastards," I cosign.

"I'm serious, Lala, where is the love? They can't say they love themselves when this type of shit happens."

"Because they don't," I tell her.

"In my mind you're either one way or the other," Dee decides.

"And I would prefer them to be straight, with no strings attached."

"Hell, I don't even know if any of us are positive, but I already feel like we are dying," Dee explains.

"Try and keep your resolve, okay, Dee," I tell her. "We didn't ask for this shit and I am praying that we're all okay."

After trying to console Dee while she blasts Mark, I convince her to call the clinic to find out the results. We need some good news. Maybe good news would stop me from hesitating to take my own test. Dee takes the cordless into my bedroom and I sit back and begin to fight back my own tears. While waiting for her return, there is another knock on my door. It's Sydney.

Sydney gives me a kiss when he walks in. I try to figure out whether or not it is a kiss of doom, but his eyes are not telling. As usual he is dressed to the nines. He takes off his hat and I take it from him and place it in my closet. He follows me as I plop back down on the couch and sits across from me not saying a word. Just staring. I know why he has stopped by and my body is getting hot again. I just hate to feel my body react this way. It is so draining. It makes it hard to keep myself under control. I want to run wild and free, trampling over anything that gets in my way, no matter how much pain I would cause. The longer Sydney sits looking at me, the more worried I become.

Finally, I say, "If you have something to say, Sydney, please go ahead 'cause I'm a big girl. I promise you I can take it."

Sydney clears his throat. "Can I have a drink of water first?"

I hand him the glass I had been drinking out of. "For God's sake, Sydney, tell me what's going on?"

Sydney looks over at Dee when she steps back into the room holding the phone. I take my attention away from Sydney. Dee is hesitant so I make a brief introduction. Everyone has finally met, after I have spoken about them to each other many times before.

I look at Dee. "So?"

She hesitates, then smiles. "All negative," she says. "We're all negative. Thank you, Jesus!"

Automatically, I think my fate is sealed in the opposite direction and I barely have enough strength to look at Sydney.

He smiles at me and says, "So is he," Sydney divulges.

When his words register, I swear out loud that I will never have sex again.

"I'm not, either," Dee says. "I don't care if I have to go to a sex store and purchase every sex toy on the market." Then she looks around. "After I get a job," she remembers.

I am so relieved. "Don't worry, Dee. If you need the money, just let me know because these men ain't worth it. Not one damn bit."

"What the hell is on these men's minds?" Dee wants to know. "Do you know how much I've worried about this shit? Running around pumping each other in the butt."

Sydney clears his throat. "Not all men," he says.

We all smile.

"Of course not you, Sydney. We need more men like you."

"Well, in my mind, that's the way I'll have to look at it. It's just too damn crazy out here. Even if you're married." Dee puts her hand over her mouth. "My girls, I have to call the girls." Dee kisses me on the cheek, then Sydney, and goes back to my room.

"It's good to see her happy," I tell Sydney.

"Well, I'm glad you're relieved, too," Sydney says.

"I'm still going to get a test," I tell him.

"Your choice, but by the information your boy gave me, I don't think you have a thing to worry about."

"My boy? Please, he's someone else's boy. It makes me wonder how many men he's slept with. It makes my body crawl."

Sydney takes out a little notebook, then moves the pages back and forth until he finds what he is looking for. "He's been with five men," he lets me know.

"Five?"

"Yes, since college."

"He told you that?"

"Told me everything I wanted to know."

Sydney's voice is so cold it makes me think that Lorenzo has been killed. I don't care either way but I still ask.

"Lala? Did you want me to kill him?"

I shrug my shoulders.

"He's not dead. Probably wishes he was, though."

I leave it at that. But I wonder what exactly he means.

"You don't have to worry about him contacting you ever again," Sydney says. "Unless you want him to."

"Of course not. Lorenzo can kiss my ass," I tell him. "So what else you have written on that pad?"

Sydney shakes his head. "Lala, I'm going to tell you straight up. Be more careful and count your blessings."

"Believe me, I am."

"You know this fool doesn't know if he's a taker or a giver."

"This is so nasty, Sydney."

"One thing I do know, he's a freak who just likes to freak. It just depends on his mood, what he wants or has."

"Disgusting."

Dee comes back in the room and chimes right into the conversation.

"Did he tell you anything about Mark?"

"Did he?... Told me everything he knew. They met at their college homecoming a few years back. Your husband propositions him. He accepts and meet back here and go at it for the last three years."

Dee says, "I think I'm going to throw up. May I ask how you got this guy to divulge so much information to you?"

"I would scare you if I did," Sydney tells Dee. "I don't want you to fear me."

Chapter 46

I t doesn't really matter to me that I have to get up the next day for work. I just want to sit with Sydney and Dee and breathe for a second; think about what our next move should be. I don't have any of that expensive liquor that Sydney drinks so he makes do drinking a strawberry daiquiri. He reminds me more than once that it seems as though he is at the Dairy Queen sipping on a slush.

"Is Mark at home with the girls now?" I ask Dee.

"No, out-of-town visiting his mother. He won't be back for a few days."

"If you want my advice, I think you and the girls should move away," I tell her.

"Believe me, if I could I would have by now. Even the police won't investigate because when they questioned the girls the night they took us from here, they would not admit to anything because he has scared them to death."

"Why don't you make him leave?" Sydney wants to know.

"You don't make Mark do anything," Dee explains.

Sydney smiles and looks at me.

"You have something in mind?" I ask him. Before he answers he pauses because my phone rings. I answer and once again there's another hang-up. It is the sixth one in the last hour or so.

Sydney continues, "Molesters don't stop. If he has made it a habit of taking advantage of them, there's a high possibility that he'll try again. It's just the way molesters act—especially when no one of authority has challenged them about it."

"Over my dead body will he ever touch me or the girls again," Dee says.

"Dee, think about it. It just might be over your dead body. Are you saying you can stop this man from doing what he's been doing whenever he wants?"

"No, I don't think I can. I mean, the only way I could would be to hurt him."

"Then you need to get on the offensive, Dee," Sydney tells her.

"And do what?"

"I would advise you to get him to a point where he feels things are getting back to normal around the house. Then when he does, he'll be ready to go ahead with business as usual."

"But I don't want that."

"That's why you have to set him up and beat him to the punch."

"Meaning?"

"Wire your house up with cameras so you'll catch him on tape. With him on tape, they'll be able to put him away for a long time and you won't have to worry about the girls refusing to make a statement to the police. They will be able to see for themselves."

"It sounds good. But cameras? I don't have money for cameras."

"But I do," Sydney lets her know.

I sit and listen while Sydney explains that with Mark out of town he can have cameras placed in the house that would never be found. At first, I thought the whole idea was a little bit too much *I Spy*, but these girls are being taken advantage of and their mother is being forced to stand by while it happens. So I just go with the flow, listen to the plan, and encourage Dee to listen to Sydney.

Their conversation becomes very graphic when Sydney begins asking questions about where in the house Mark would molest the girls. Dee tells him. Mark would take them into his bedroom or theirs, but there wasn't a specific place because Mark had become so cocky about his actions. Sydney talks Dee into letting him come over the next day while the kids are at school, so they would be unaware of the cameras which would keep them safe. While they talk, I can tell Dee is hesitant but she doesn't have a choice. I assure her that Sydney is a man of his word and before she leaves, she gives Sydney

her address and tells him to meet her there at nine in
the morning.

After Dee leaves for home and Sydney finishes giving
some instructions to a guy named Russell over the phone,
I zero into him without delay and bring up Nancy.

"Sydney, I think Nancy is a little apprehensive about
your feelings toward her."

"She tell you that?"

"Not in so many words, but I get the feeling she believes
you don't care for her as much as you used to."

"Why? Because I told her I wanted more space?"

"Possibly," I clarify.

"I really don't get it. I never told Nancy that I was
thinking about leaving her or finding someone new."

"But you told her that you felt like having an open relationship after all the years you two have been together."

"Yes, I did do that."

"Well, you opened up a very big can of worms, Sydney."

Sydney tries to look beyond our conversation as though
he doesn't want to visit the topic.

"You're going to have to talk to her, Sydney."

"About?"

"About your relationship. I can give you a woman's
point of view on being in a relationship and love even
though you've known Nancy a hell of a lot longer than
I have."

"Oh, this is some universal shit?"

"Worldwide," I let him know. "It's plain and simple, women are women. We would like men to talk to us and let us know how you feel. Just getting space from a person means oodles to a woman, trust me."

"That's it, hunh? Just letting her know how I feel about her? That does the trick?"

"Take Keith, for example. If he would have just let me know in the beginning that he and Adria were sneaking around having sex or whatever; even let me know that he didn't think I was the one for him. It would have possibly given me back some of the years I wasted with him so that I could find a man who wanted the same thing that I did. And look at this fool, Lorenzo. He didn't say one word about being on the DL. He got what he wanted from me. Used me, to put it mildly, then turns around and tells me after the fact, after he could have infected me with some shit."

Sydney sighs. "So you think I should talk to her?"

"I sure do. Tell her what's really on your mind, Sydney."

"Lala, telling Nancy what is on my mind got us in this little situation that we're in now."

"Understood, but I think it might help a bit, go more indepth about your feelings. Do you know she's seeing a psychiatrist, Sydney?"

Sydney sits up a bit in his chair. "A psychiatrist? What the hell for? For how long?"

"Told me she was seeing him for a while now. Said

he'd been giving her advice on your marriage and even told me that he felt your marriage was in a crisis."

"So, that's where she got that bullshit?"

"What do you mean?"

"The other night, during dinner, she just started bawling for no reason. I asked her what the problem was and she relayed the doctor's feelings to me as they were her own."

"What did you say to her?"

"It was strange. But she didn't seem like herself and I think I remember asking her where'd she get such an idea because it couldn't have been farther from the truth."

"So, you don't feel like that yourself?"

"Hell no. Absolutely not. Lala, people go through things. Men go through things just like women do. I only asked her for something that I thought I wanted. I see men my age sometimes with a different lady on their arm every night. I thought I wanted to be a part of that and keep her, too. And for nothing else—just for conversation's sake."

"Oh, the younger-woman syndrome?"

"Call it what you want. But you're a witness that what I wanted was just a thought. Hell, a fantasy, if you'd like. I have never thought of myself being without Nancy. It's just that plain and simple."

I smile at Sydney because I know he really means what he's said to me. I remember he actually had this and didn't even take it, when I offered.

"So this doctor? What's his name, who is he?"

I am hesitant to even entertain his question. "Sydney, please don't tell Nancy I said anything."

"Never."

"Well, she didn't give me his name. She just told me that he was a black man."

Sydney chuckles. "A black man?"

"Yes, what's wrong with that?"

"You know niggas. Always putting salt in game for their own best interests."

After all that has happened to me in the last few months, I cannot help but to see his point. "So you'll talk to her?" I want to know.

"Sure, I will and soon."

Chapter 47

The continuous ringing of my phone keeps me from getting any decent sleep tonight. There is a call around three in the morning. Whoever it is is definitely getting on my last nerve. I "star sixty-nine" through the darkness each time it happens but the number continues to turn up private. The calls are beginning to scare me. After all this time I am still not used to living alone. If I would have had a man I'd have just snuggled up in his arms and not let the calls bother me. But I don't and I can't, so I basically go back to sleep. I decide that more than likely it's Lorenzo making me uncomfortable from a distance since Sydney would beat his ass if he ever contacted me again.

The next morning at work I'm not as rested as I would like. I have a very busy day in front of me. But I am on an emotional high because I am well. I am sure my motivation level is going to be enough to carry me through, especially after getting the good news from Sydney. I am so relieved that I can move on with my life. But the first thing I do is call my doctor for a complete check-up.

It is already close to eleven and Nancy has called three times. The first time I am in a meeting, the second in another meeting, and the third, I am sitting in a meeting trying to decide when we would have another meeting. After lunch, I finally get an opportunity to call Nancy and her assistant patches me right through.

"You rang?"

"And how are you…?"

"Things are moving fast and furious," I tell her. "Matter of fact, I have another meeting in ten minutes."

"Well, I won't keep you. Guess who's going on a shopping spree to New York City with Sydney…"

"Oh really now…"

"Yes, indeed!"

It is so good to hear that Sydney is taking the offensive in his relationship with Nancy. I knew all along that he had it in him. It's probably what made me sort of interested in him when we first met. "So when are you leaving?"

"Said he's getting the tickets tonight so I won't know until then."

"Girl, there is no place better to get your shop on than in the city! I am so proud of you two…"

"Isn't it exciting?"

"Plus, you get that one-on-one quality time and a chance to do what lovers do."

"Which is just what we need," Nancy affirms.

"You're absolutely right."

Nancy pauses a bit. "Thanks, Lala."

I am a bit confused but don't get a chance to tell her.

"I know you probably prodded him into doing this," she says.

"Nancy, to be honest, I didn't."

"Really?"

"Serious. As far as I know, this was all his doing. Maybe he's coming back around."

"Well, I certainly hope so. I've really been knocking my brain around on how to get things back to the way they were with Sydney. I've been completely stressing."

"Relationships grind on you, I understand."

"Don't I know it? It's gotten so bad that my doctor gave me a prescription for antidepressants."

"For what?"

"He said the pressure behind this all has stifled my ability to make decisions in my life."

"What's he mean by that, Nancy?"

"I guess about the divorce. Wanting it. Then not wanting it. Just being stressed about that whole thing, I guess."

"I thought you already decided against that?"

"I did, but the doctor doesn't seem as though I look at the circumstances with a clear head. He thinks I'm holding on to Sydney because I'm afraid of moving on without him. In his words, my marriage is doomed to fail—*a classic case*."

"Hello, you guys have only been together—what… forever? So what does he think you should do?"

"He refuses to tell me," Nancy says. "Says it should be my decision on what direction to move my life in."

"Seems like he's telling you what to do indirectly, Nancy. So these antidepressants are supposed to do the trick?"

"I guess," Nancy says. "I have to admit, so far they've really helped me to relax and not be so uptight about what's going on in our relationship."

I am rushed for time so I don't really have a lot of time to tell Nancy how I feel about taking medication to deal with life problems. I definitely am not a fan. If I were with all the shit going on in my life, at the time I would be like a walking zombie. Medications for anything scare the hell out of me. I have come to a point where I think everyone in America needs something in order to help them deal with what they created. I'm not knocking Nancy for taking the drugs, but I think I know her well enough to conclude that she doesn't need any drugs. In my eyes she has her life in order and is definitely a lady that a lot of black women aspire to be.

As I finish with Nancy, I notice an urgent-message note on my desk from Dee so I stand up, grab my note pad—which is quickly becoming filled with show notes—and dial Dee's number as fast as I can.

"Hey, Dee," I say to her as I look on my desk for the show's shot chart that I had been given earlier in the morning.

"Lala, Sydney is here and I don't think this is a wise decision to put these cameras in the house," she says very rushed.

"Dee? What are you talking about?"

"I'm just saying. This shit looks serious," she says.

"Dee, look, it is serious."

"I know, but I don't know if I want to do this. It just seems so violating."

"Violating? Mark is the one who is violating."

Dee's voice trails off. "I know…"

"Besides, how else are you going to get from underneath Mark and stop him from what he's doing? You and I both know it's just a matter of time before he starts to feel comfortable with you being back in that house, and it's going to be business as usual."

"Well, how long? How long do I have to live with these cameras, Lala?"

"Dee, as long as it takes. Don't lose focus. All we want is Mark away from you and the kids as soon as possible."

Dee pauses. "Yeah you're right. But they better hurry up and leave. These guys are making me nervous."

I ask Dee to hand Sydney the phone.

"Yeah?" I can tell by Sydney's voice he has a crew over Dee's getting things set up as fast as possible.

"How are things going?"

"Would have been finished by now," Sydney lets me

know. "But when I got here, Dee didn't want to go through with it. But we're about ten to fifteen minutes from being finished and then we are out of here."

"Dee's pretty scared, Sydney. Are you sure he won't be able to notice the cameras?"

"Lala, my guys are good at what they do. You should already know that," he confirms with the confidence you like to hear from a man.

I smile because I remember how they took care of Lorenzo. "Okay, well, please reassure Dee before you leave."

"Don't worry. I will."

"Oh, call me later," I tell Sydney right before I hang up.

"Sounds serious?"

"Not too, but it's about your trip to New York," I punch.

"Oh you heard?"

"Sure did, Mr. Romantic."

Chapter 48

hings run smoothly the next couple of weeks. I am able to settle into my job and develop my daily routine. I even do something that I haven't in such a very long time—I go to church. But I struggle to stay the entire service. For me, it is like going to a club or a show. I have always been a prayerful person and continue to pray through all of my changes. But I think that assembling in a church will give me that added boost that I need to continue my progress in my life. But the atmosphere from the time I step out of my car and walk into the church is the same feeling when I was fresh out of school going out to clubs or a night on the town looking to flirt.

There is no mistaking my feelings. The women—those who sit alone and some with men by their sides—look at me as though I am someone else they have to contend with to find a man instead of saying hello to me and welcoming me to the church. The ladies sitting with men would find a way to shoot me a dirty look as to say their man was off limits as if I would take him away. After a while, I can't take it any longer. I realize that I would rather continue praying alone in my own home in peace and quiet until I find a church that is able to feed me what I am looking for instead of nasty, dry looks from females.

To put more salt in the wound, the high, recognizable preacher, who's on television almost every day, surprises me and some others who are listening to his message. He tells the congregation that if he didn't have a job and his wife did, he would go to her job every time she was paid, take her check and go put it in his bank. Then when she gets home, he might even "give her some." Then he clarifies that he's not talking about money. It makes me think even preachers, supposedly the most holy of them all, have game.

I also find the time to finally make sure for once and for all that I have not contracted anything from Lorenzo. Just the thought that his sperm had a chance to swim inside me when his condom broke was enough to make me puke. By the grace of God, the test came back negative. But just taking the test was enough to actually scare me straight.

When I went to take my test, I couldn't help but wonder how many other women sitting in the waiting area with me also were there to take an HIV test. Not only that—how many of the women there were not as fortunate as I was? How many had children and now had to not only fight the battle of being single with kids but struggle through life taking care of them and dealing with a man who can't decide his sexual orientation. I am able to read some information that the doctor gave me concerning contracting AIDS and the statistics almost paralyze me.

Then it is apparent to me why I get all the cold stares at church. I am also in constant contact with Dee. And as Sydney promised he had the cameras set up. Every day when Mark would go to work, Dee would check them to make sure he hadn't molested the girls. Dee seemed as though she was happy we talked her into getting the cameras. The girls were back in their routine and my boy Sean and his dog were into any and everything every chance they got.

As always, just when I think things are under control, all hell begins to break loose.

"I know, you're surprised to see me, right?" are the first words Sydney says to me when I walk into my office on one of my busiest days.

Hell yes, I am surprised because he is supposed to be in New York with his wife but he is sitting behind my desk. As far as I knew they'd already been gone for a couple of days. At this point I am sure they were more than likely getting their love and reconciliation on.

"Sydney? What are you doing here? How come you're not in the Big Apple?"

"I didn't scare you, did I?" Sydney stands and helps me put my things down on my desk. I am holding my coffee mug, briefcase, and a stack of scripts.

"You scared the shit out of me, Sydney. What gives?"

He has a definite look of concern on his face. "She left, Lala."

"Left? What are you talking about?"

"We were in New York having a nice time. Or at least I thought we were...then all of a sudden, Nancy just wasn't Nancy."

Sydney realizes how confused I am. I don't know what the hell he is talking about. I turn my coffee mug up, take a sip, and motion for him to tell me more.

"Okay, we took the flight to New York. Checked in the hotel and went shopping for most of the first day. That night, we had dinner and after I told Nancy how sorry I was for taking her through all the shit the last couple of months, her whole attitude changed."

"Changed, like how?"

"She just seemed as though being with me was all too much. I don't know. Everything I said to her seemed to upset her, and I couldn't figure out why and she didn't offer to tell me. The next morning when I thought she was down in the gym of the hotel working out, I found a note next to the coffee pot telling me that she couldn't do this anymore."

"So, where did she go?"

"I don't have any idea, Lala. I waited around the hotel to see if she was coming back or not. When she didn't show, I got a flight back home."

"So you haven't seen her?"

Sydney shakes his head no. "Nor have I spoken with her. I called back here when I was in New York to have one of the fellows keep an eye on her place to see if she made it back home, but there was no sign of her."

"Is there anyplace you know of she would go?"

"I don't know. Nancy has a lot of friends, but I don't see her reaching out to them for a place to stay. I was hoping she would have called you."

I sit down in my chair and look across at Sydney after telling him I don't have a clue where Nancy could be. Sydney is normally still and reserved, but he looks very anxious and will not stop rubbing his hands together because he is so agitated. "Did you call the police?" I want to know.

"I don't like the police, Lala," he says firmly.

"I know but, maybe you should?"

"For what? Tell them my wife's gone and then have their asses all over me?"

I can see his point. There is no way they are going to give him space after they find out Nancy is missing because that's how they do. But still she is missing. "I think you should call anyway," I tell him.

He looks up at me. "Really?"

"Yes, really."

Chapter 49

I put all my work on my desk, cancel my meetings for the day, and I'm off with Sydney after he thinks there is a good chance that Nancy is over her sister's house in Macon, Georgia. Until he mentions her, I have forgotten Nancy has a sister because she has only mentioned her to me once or twice. Sydney promises that he will call the police if Nancy is not there. I agree with him that it is a good idea. We leave my office and start down I-75 South in Sydney's car. He turns an hour's drive into forty minutes saying as little as possible along the way.

I have never been to Macon before. When we arrive, my first thoughts are it was really not too much to it. It looks to be a small town filled with people who love Georgia but not the traffic and congestion of Atlanta. Sydney makes his way downtown and in no time we are driving through a neighborhood that has the most beautiful old houses that I'd ever seen in my life. They are huge and seem to take up an entire corner and then some. Sydney makes a wrong turn on one of the streets but quickly gets his bearings. He pulls into a driveway of a gorgeous white house that looks from the outside to have at least twelve bedrooms inside.

Despite all the stress Sydney is going through, he still hasn't forgotten his manners and opens my car door for me. It is a very short walk up to the front door of the house because the driveway allows for cars to pull close to the entrance.

I like the fact that the house doesn't have much grass in front of it. It reminds me so much of the huge mansions I once saw in Miami when I vacationed there with Keith.

Sydney looks at me, takes a deep breath, and knocks on the door.

When the door is opened, there is a lady standing inside who no doubt is related to Nancy. There is no hiding the family lineage. Her eyes, her stance, her bone structure and her skin tone are similar to Nancy. But then she opens her mouth after giving us a long and lazy glancing over.

"Sydney." She pauses. Her voice is much deeper than Nancy's and it is apparent she has some street about herself. She looks at me. "And you are?"

Sydney cuts me off before I can tell her my name. "Sheila, this is Lala," he tells her. "You have a minute?"

"Depends," she says back.

I don't know exactly what is going on between Sydney and Sheila, but I can tell one thing: She did not enjoy that we were at her front door.

"Can we at least come inside?" Sydney wants to know.

Sheila exhales hard, sort of rolls her eyes, then steps aside so we can enter. I follow Sydney and he takes about seven steps inside, then looks around as we stand inside the huge foyer. I glance around without trying to seem like I am being nosey. The one thing that catches my attention is how the sunlight shines inside the huge windows near the top of the house.

Inside the foyer, there are chairs next to a tree that has been planted inside the house. Sydney sits down in one while I sit in the other.

Sheila stands looking at us with her hands on her hips.

"What's wrong with Nancy?" she wants to know.

Sydney crosses his legs. "You tell me?" he asks.

Sheila's eyes wander.

"Do you know where she is?"

Sheila looks at Sydney like he is a fool or something. "Why would I know where she is? She's your wife."

Sydney drops his head, then looks back up at Sheila. "Sheila, I don't know where she is. I thought she might have come here."

Sheila is wearing a men's button-down shirt over a T-shirt and she takes out a cigarette from the pocket. She doesn't speak until she lights up and gets a taste of the menthol. "So you came here looking for her?"

"That's right," Sydney says.

"Why here?"

"I didn't know where else to look. Besides, she's your sister."

"Yeah, but me and Nancy haven't talked in weeks."

I am beginning to get uncomfortable from all the looks she is throwing my way.

"So she's not here, hunh?" Sydney wants to know again.

"Nope."

Sydney sits back in his chair as if he is deflated.

Sheila looks at me. "So you're Lala…" Her eyes are hard on me, then she turns to Sydney.

I don't like her tone one bit but I tell her I am.

"Nancy called here a few months back and mentioned you," she says.

I look at Sydney. "Me?"

"Sure did. Told me Sydney had him a new friend. Name was Lala. So I take it that was you?"

"I suppose…"

"Yeah, Nancy wasn't too happy when she called." Sheila looks at Sydney. "She was bummed out by the fact that her husband had been spending time with a younger woman."

Sydney stands up as if ready to leave. "I thought you hadn't talked to her?"

"I didn't talk, nigga; I listened to my sister when she had something troubling her mind," she says.

"And you haven't talked to her since?"

Sheila takes another puff from her smoke. "I told you no. But when she comes home, you call and let me know."

Sydney promises Sheila he will, then we walk right past Sheila and out the door.

Sydney is quiet until we are back on the highway heading back to Atlanta.

"Sometimes that woman can work my last nerve," he says.

"What was her problem?"

"She's always been like that as long as I can remember."

"Any particular reason, why?"

Sydney takes a long pause. "She's a few years younger than Nancy and when their parents died, Nancy took care of her for a few years. Hell, we both did."

"Not a good experience, hunh?"

"Fuckin' nightmare. All she wanted to do is smoke, drink, and party. We barely got her outta high school. The house she's living in was her parents'. Luckily, they had some money saved up when they died and she lives off of it—hasn't worked a day in her life."

"Well, she obviously didn't like me, that's for sure."

"Don't let her get to you. She's not even an issue."

"So what're you going to do now?" I ask him.

"Guess I'll go back and let the police know that she's missing. I just don't have a clue as to where she could be."

Sydney becomes stone quiet. I try to keep things as calm as I can, bringing up every other subject that I thought he might be interested in to ease his mind, but it doesn't work. Sydney sideswipes my conversations and starts to tell me about the time Nancy didn't call him for days when they were younger. He almost seems as though he enjoys telling the story but I can tell his pain is real. He explains that he didn't think she would return to him when she lost their baby the first and only time she had ever become pregnant.

Sydney talks about Nancy as though she is his life, and I come to the conclusion she is. We both want to know if she is okay in the worst way.

Chapter 50

B y now things are moving hella fast but slow in the same fashion. It's passing us by but we are hearing nothing and know even less about Nancy. I have Sydney drop me off at the office. By the looks of all the notes and messages sprawled on my desk, it is apparent that the scheduled meetings went on without me and were very productive.

I don't feel much like working with Nancy on my mind so I begin to gather some items to take back home to work. With my arms full, I am two seconds from turning out the light in my office when the phone rings. I decide to answer it but there is no response. I place the phone back down, take a few steps toward the door, then the phone rings again. When I pick up this time, I say hello three times before I faintly hear a voice and figure out who it is.

"Nancy?" There is another pause. While I wait to hear her voice again, I put my things back down on my desk and place my ear extra tight to the receiver.

"I can't take it anymore…" Nancy's voice is very sluggish and tired.

"You okay, Nancy? Where are you?"

"It all depends on what you call okay," she says.

I sit down in my chair. "Nancy, where are you?" My voice is forceful because I want Nancy to know right away that we are concerned about her.

"I'm okay…"

"No, where are you? Why'd you leave Sydney in New York?"

"Lala, hold on a second, okay, hon?"

I hear Nancy put down the phone and there is a faint sound of running water being poured into a glass. She picks up the phone again after a minute or so. "I left New York because it didn't feel right. That's why I left."

"Didn't feel right?"

"The whole trip, Lala, it seemed Sydney was trying to appease me. It was evident that he was going through the motions to make me feel better for my sake and not our relationship or our future."

"Nancy, I don't think that's so. Sydney loves you and he's going crazy not knowing if you're okay or not. Are you still in New York?"

"No, I'm here," she says.

"Good, where are you so I can come see you?"

"It's no need for that, Lala. Besides, I wouldn't be good company."

"It doesn't matter, I just want to make sure you're okay," I tell her. I am looking down at the new phone she had put in my office to check the number on the caller ID. The number is private. Nancy doesn't respond to me so I want to keep talking with her. I am hoping that she will open up and let me in. "So this staying-away thing that you're doing. How long are you going to need before you go back to Sydney?" Then I kind of chuckled. "Not to mention getting back to work."

"I don't know, Lala. I just need to get away for a few days. I have a lot of soul searching to do. There's just so much to think about at this point. You know, half the time I don't think men realize what type of anguish they put us through."

I can definitely relate to Nancy. "Shit, it's more than half the time."

Nancy laughs a bit. "Okay, I'll give you that one. But they really don't, Lala…"

Nancy's voice trails off. It becomes lower and slower but the difference of tone is not enough for me to really question it. I'm thinking she might be turning the television or something.

"Oh, you don't have to convince me, Nancy. I, for one, have sworn off men for at least the next ten years."

"Ten years? What are you talking about, Lala."

I still hadn't told Nancy what I'd gone through and since things were resolved, I feel like it's okay to fill her in. "Well, you remember the guy I told you about that I was kind of seeing?"

"Lorenzo, right?"

"Yeah, it hurts to just hear his name," I say.

"What about him?"

"Well, he was on the DL."

"What type of pills are those?…" Nancy inquires.

"Nancy. They aren't pills. It means when a man sleeps with other men without anyone knowing about it."

"Really?"

"Absolutely, that's what he was doing."

"Girl, that's nasty," she decides.

"Isn't it? So, I've decided to just love me for me because I cannot continue to put myself out on a limb for some fool to take my life and give me some type of disease that won't go away."

"Just like I said, Lala, they just don't care about us anymore."

"I can't say all men, Nancy. I know firsthand that Sydney is worried sick about you."

"I'm sure he is. But my therapist thinks Sydney will continue to want his cake and eat it, too."

"That's ridiculous, Nancy. Does this man even know Sydney?"

"No, they've never met but he said that he's met plenty of men like him."

Chapter 51

By the time our conversation is finished, there's no doubt that Nancy is not the same confident, self-assured woman I'd first met not long ago at dinner. I rush to call Sydney to let him know that we have spoken. After I tell him my concerns he feels it's time to finally meet Nancy's therapist to find out all he knows.

"So, she didn't tell you where she was staying?" Sydney wants to know.

"All she said was that she was back here."

"Are you sure she said she needed something stronger to take?"

"Said something about a prescription that needed to be made stronger. Did you know she was taking anything?"

"Not a clue. I couldn't tell you what or how many. I had no idea."

"Sydney, are you sure you want me to go see this doctor with you?"

"Of course I do. I need you right now, like never before."

Sydney didn't say too much past that. He does ask about Dee but I don't think it is because he is so much concerned about her as it is trying to get Nancy off his mind for a while. His asking about her gives me the idea to call her, to see how she is doing while we ride over to see the doctor. Just my luck Mark answers the phone. I ask to speak with Dee and when he realizes it's me, it's as though he is thinking about hanging up in my ear. He sighs and Dee must have been sitting next to him because I don't hear him call for her to answer the phone.

She answers.

"Hey, Dee."

"Hello…"

"I know you can't talk much. I just wanted to check in and see how things were going?"

"They're fine." Dee's tone of voice hadn't changed.

"Look, I've been really busy but I plan on making it over there to see you and the kids as soon as I can, okay?"

"Don't worry, Lala. I know you will when you get a chance."

Dee's voice doesn't sit too well with me. It is like Mark was standing directly over her monitoring everything she is saying.

Sydney turns into the parking lot of the doctors.

"Well, I have to go now," I tell her. "I'll call you a little later."

"Okay, and Lala, I won't be able to go shopping with you tomorrow. The girls want me to hang out with them, so I guess we'll have to reschedule."

❖❖❖

We arrive at the doctor's and Sydney asks the receptionist if her boss is available. Of course she tells him no, after she realizes he doesn't have an appointment and is carrying a hell of an attitude in his front pocket. But Sydney doesn't turn and walk away after his initial request is denied. He is aggressive. Barraging her with questions. Doesn't take her "I don't know attitude," and definitely doesn't budge when she mentions security. The receptionist can't handle Sydney. After a while, the doctor is listening to what is going on outside his office because he finally comes out to see what really is going on.

When he struts out of his office, there is no denying that Mr. Man thinks he is the shit. He's not wearing a suit jacket. Just a dress shirt with black pants and shoes that look to be of very good quality. He stands about an inch or two shorter than Sydney and when he puts his hand out to greet Sydney, Sydney looks him off and tells him directly that he wants to talk to him about Nancy.

The doctor looks over at his receptionist to silence her after she tries to tell him that she's already denied Sydney's request. Soon after, the doctor invites us in without another word from Sydney.

We walk inside and I notice the painted walls, a light beige on one side of the room and a darker green on the far wall behind his desk. The furniture is nothing to get excited about but I look for *the chair*. I notice it on the far side of the room sitting next to a coffee table. It looks just like I imagined. Long enough to lie down on and big enough to sit up straight comfortably in.

Dr. Diggs invites us to sit. He walks behind his desk, slides down into his chair, then asks Sydney how he can help him.

Sydney is straight to the point. "You've been seeing my wife?"

The doctor's facial expressions are as though he knew Sydney would come at him straightforward, no chaser.

"I didn't hear your answer," Sydney adds. "Her name is Nancy."

"I usually don't…"

"But you will talk about one of your patients today," Sydney interrupts.

I look over at Sydney. He is sitting calmly. Legs crossed, hands folded. But he hasn't taken his eyes off of Dr. Diggs since he sat down. Sydney is focused on getting down to what this man had been feeding his wife.

The doctor displays a smile. He isn't cool, no matter how hard he tries to be.

"Look, there's no reason for any hostilities. I am very aware of who you are and have no problems telling you what you want to know," he bargains.

"Well, let's get down to it then," Sydney says back.

The doctor gives Sydney the floor with a hand gesture, then he makes his tie and collar shirt even and nice.

"How long has my wife been coming here?"

The doctor looks at me before he answers.

"She's my niece," Sydney tells him.

"She's not Lala?" the doctor asks.

Sydney looks at me and is surprised.

"And if she was?"

"From what I've heard about you, I just wouldn't be surprised that you brought her along," he says. "If in fact, that's who she is."

"So she's Lala. Now what?"

"It just makes things a little more clear," he says.

I have to butt in now, because I'm in the Kool-Aid and didn't even know it.

"How so?" I try to find out.

"Puts names to faces. You're exactly how Nancy has described you."

"Why would she be in here talking about Lala?" Sydney questions.

The doctor's sarcasm comes at the wrong time. "You of all people should know the reason behind that."

"You wait one gotdamn minute," Sydney tells him. "I don't know anything at all. The only thing I know is that you've been seeing my wife, and as I understand it, prescribing medicine that I was not even aware she was taking."

Dr. Diggs takes offense to Sydney's tone. "Your wife is battling depression, sir."

"Depression? What are you talking about?"

"If I might, it began with your request to get a little space from your wife. In my line of work, we call it a mid-life crisis."

Sydney doesn't respond to the doctor; I'm glad that he doesn't.

"Your wife is very delicate. She's one of the most caring women that I have met in a long time. She has a conscience. She cares about family and even though she wasn't able to give you children, which she is so very sorry for, believe it or not, she has lived her entire life to please you." The doctor realizes he has Sydney's undivided attention now. "Nancy only wanted to please you and I'm sorry to say that you took something out of her that has been very difficult for me to recover."

"So you started with the prescriptions?"

"I didn't have any other choice. Your wife has a very stressful job. She's a top-level executive and needed something to take the edge off."

"Well, have you seen her lately?" I ask him.

The doctor looks me over before he answers. "Yes, I have."

Sydney uncrosses his legs. I ask the doctor when.

"Earlier today," he confides.

"Did you change her prescription?"

"How did you know about that?"

"She called me. She told me that she wanted something stronger to help her cope with whatever you were telling her."

"I didn't think she needed anything stronger," the doctor says. "It's good to know she's home and reaching out, though."

Sydney is confused and so am I. Sydney tells him, "She's not home."

Dr. Diggs looks baffled. "She told me before she left that she was going home."

We sit with Dr. Diggs for another twenty minutes before we leave.

"I don't like him, Lala. He definitely pushed my buttons."

"He rubbed me the wrong way, too."

"Motherfucker knew too much of my business, Lala. No man should know that much about another man's personal business. I don't care, doctor or not."

"He did seem to know a lot about what was going on in your household."

"When Nancy gets home, we're going to have a long talk. I had no idea she was telling this guy our business like that."

"Well, at least she told him she was going home."

His demeanor changes a bit. "Yeah, that's good news in itself."

"Do me a favor when she does, Sydney. Be gentle with her. Let her talk and try to understand where she is coming from, okay?"

Sydney thinks for a good while. "You don't have to worry. I'll do just that."

Chapter 52

Later that night, I'm sort of sleep but awake completely when I hear pounding at my door. At first I'm thinking the pounding is courtesy of the early morning Georgia storm. But when I look out my window, I notice Sydney's car parked in my driveway with the headlights on and windshield wipers going berserk fighting the rain. Although I'm sure it's Sydney, I ask if it's him through the door. He lets me know it is, so I let him in. He steps inside dripping wet and eyes bloodshot red.

"Lala, I found her," he says.

"Nancy? You mean she's home?"

"No, the police called."

"Police?"

"They found Nancy in a rental in the parking lot at the zoo."

"Sydney…"

"She's dead, Lala. They are telling me that my Nancy took her own life."

Before I can reach out for Sydney he is leaning up

against my wall, and sliding down to the floor with his head in his hands sobbing uncontrollably.

I'm shock-locked in my house for the next three days. I am paralyzed and stunned at the thought of Nancy taking her own life. It is a very helpless feeling to see the car she was found in flashed over and over again on television. It isn't until the day of Nancy's funeral that I am able to get out of the bed. I have to call a cab to take me to the funeral because when I get behind the wheel of my car, I don't have the strength to drive to see Nancy placed into the ground.

It is still raining outside and I take it as a sign that God is crying out loud from the loss of Nancy. Things like this are not supposed to happen to people like her. It is apparent by all those who are in attendance at the funeral that she was very well liked. Over five-hundred people standing outside in the rain with her as they begin to place her body back down into the earth. I have so much difficulty even looking at Sydney as he sits as close as he can to the casket as it is being lowered in the ground.

There's not a soul who can tell me he didn't love Nancy with all his heart. The man that I knew to be so strong is at his weakest point, one that broke my heart to witness. I can't help but think about the letter Sydney let me read that Nancy left for him. Even though she took her own life, it was beautiful that she could love her man so much. She told Sydney that she loved him with every ounce of her blood. It was the only reason she decided to take her life because she could not stand to live with the possibilities of her not being the only woman on his mind.

After the funeral I'm at home. The house is quiet and I'm at a loss for words or any type of reasoning behind Nancy's tragic death. I do spend a while wondering if she really thought I was ever a threat to her marriage; even though I thought we were clear on the subject.

There's a knock at my door shortly past nine. I don't even look out to see who it is. I don't care—I just open the door and see Sydney standing. Numb, drunk, still wearing his black suit holding a bottle of Scotch.

He slurs, "Can I come the fuck in, Lala?"

I help him in, wondering how in the hell he made it driving over, then guide him into a chair.

I am standing with my arms folded, trying to imagine what type of pain he's in. After a few minutes, he finally speaks.

"You know I loved her, Lala."

I can't answer. Seeing Sydney this way saddens me and brings me to tears.

"Answer me, Lala. Don't you know I loved her?"

I sit on my knees beside the chair, then wipe my eyes. The lightning and storm sounds as though it's back full force. I can see flashes from my window's reflection shine on Sydney's face. "Yes, I know you loved Nancy, Sydney. There's no denying that."

"But I should have told her, Lala. I should have told Nancy I loved her more than anything else in the world."

"I think she knew that, Sydney."

"Yeah, but I never told her. I hadn't told her I loved her in almost five years. Five gotdamn years."

I don't know what to say to Sydney because what he is telling me is foul. I don't want to believe it coming from the man I believe to have so much polish and class. "So, you never talked to her like I told you to, either, did you, Sydney?"

Sydney never answered or moved when the lightning flashed across his face again.

His silence angers me and I yell out to him, "You never fuckin' told her, did you!"

My emotions run over and I begin to cry out loud. Then I start to pound on his chest with all the strength I have left, until my head falls from exhaustion on Sydney's chest while the reflection from the lightning beams off both our grieving bodies.

Chapter 53

I wait a few more days and attempt to drag myself into work. The whole place has been shocked at Nancy's death. But I believe it's my duty to her to stay focused and at least attempt to do the job she was gracious enough to give to me.

I still don't have the strength to drive yet. So, I call a car to take me back and forth for at least the first week. I plan to go see Sydney each day after work. Even though I am mad at him for playing a big part in Nancy's emotional state, I can't totally blame him because we both agreed the medication prescribed by her doctor is what probably took her over the top. There's just no way to understand a woman's breaking point. But I promised myself I would always respect a woman's limit.

In the backseat of the car looking out during the ride home, I begin to wonder how I can make my life matter. For some strange reason, things that have happened in my life the last few months are resonating perfectly clearly in my memory at a rapid pace...Keith, Adria, Lorenzo, meeting Sydney, and Nancy, her death, then all of a sudden Dee and the kids. When I focus on Dee and the kids, it strikes my mind that the last time I had spoken with Dee over the phone, she mentioned that we had planned to go shopping. But I realize we never did plan to go shopping together.

Out of pure speculation I ask the driver to take me to Dee's and to wait for me in front of the house. It is a little past nine but it seems much later because of the darkness of the clouds and the rain that is now stop and go trying to fade. I scurry up to the front porch and use the handle on the outside of the door to knock. It takes a while but I notice a black hand pull back the small curtain attached to the door frame. Then the tumblers of the locks to the door begin to unlock. Mark has answered. His eyes are bloodshot red and he is wearing a T-shirt and faded jeans without any shoes. He stares at me as he holds the door open.

I don't wait for him to say anything. "Hello, Mark, is Dee here?"

It is really difficult to hear him over the rain hitting the house and the pavement behind me. "She's not here," he says.

But I don't believe him. Something about Mark's eyes is full of deceit. His body language is telling something totally different. Maybe it's the way he's positioning his body in the door and holding it with his hand. "Well, can you tell me when she will be back?"

Mark smirks. "Lala, right? I don't know when she'll be back. But when she comes back, if…she comes back, I'll be sure to tell her you stopped by."

"I don't understand, what do you mean, *if?* Does she still live here?"

"You know, you have always asked way too many questions for my taste."

"Well, I'm…"

He cuts me off. "Look, she's not here."

I have never professed to being a private detective but something isn't right with Mark. He seems as though he has a million things running through his mind. Right before I am going to turn around and leave, he makes the mistake of stepping back and opening the door far enough for me to see inside. That is when I see Sean. He looks at me briefly, then at his father with the fear of death in his eyes.

Mark shouts at him, "Didn't I tell you not to move!"

Sean looks at me again, then runs into one of the rooms out of my sight. Mark tries to close the door where I can't see inside again. He smiles. It's more like a snarl and I take a few steps back from the door. Mark looks at me, then at the car and driver parked in his driveway.

"You know what…I think she'll be back in a few minutes. Wanna come in and wait for her?"

Right then I realize something inside isn't right. I don't turn my back on Mark. I find my way off his porch while he stares down at me, then shuts the front door again. When I get back into the car, I tell the driver to pull around the corner and that's when I call the police.

Chapter 54

Within minutes two squad cars are in front of the house. I am sitting in back of one of the cruisers and a white officer tells me his name is Houston along with his partner, Samuel, who is black. They are asking questions about what I thought was happening inside before they even attempt to go see for themselves.

"Are you sure we should be sitting right in front of the house?" I want to know.

The officer taking the notes and writing the report tips his hat upward and turns to me from the front seat. "Ma'am, don't worry. If something is going down inside, sometimes just the sight of our presence makes the most unruly bastards think twice about what they intend on doing."

He doesn't soothe or calm me. All I can think of, is already losing one friend and I can't even stand the thought of something happening to Dee, the girls, and Sean. I'm feeling terrible that I didn't catch Dee's hint on the phone, and I tell the officers all about it.

"So there's one black man inside?" the officer wants clarified.

I nod yes.

"And when you went to the door, he seemed agitated?"

"Yes, he looked like he was having a very bad day. You know, like he was hiding something."

"Tell me about these allegations of molestation again."

"There's nothing to tell. This man had been molesting his daughters, by his wife's account."

"And she had cameras installed to catch him in the act?"

"Yes, yes, she did." About ten seconds later, my cell phone rings and I fumble through my purse to answer it. "Hello?"

"Lala?"

"Dee?"

I motion with my hands to the officer that Dee is on the phone.

"Dee, where are you? Are you okay?"

"Lala, Mark says if the police even step into the yard, he's going to kill us all."

Just to hear Dee say those words almost makes me faint. "Okay, okay, I'll tell them, Dee. Is everyone inside okay?"

Dee manages to tell me "yes" before the sound of a dial tone is in my ear.

Ten minutes later, the scene in front of the house is unimaginable. There are two SWAT teams, numerous police cars, and a mobile tactical unit that I'm now sitting in with officers who are setting up to deal with what they are calling a hostage situation. I look around the trailer and it's as if I'm the only one inside who is scared as hell, as to what is about to happen. After I give all the information that I know to the officers who have taken over, I sit in the corner and wait for them to do their jobs. After about thirty minutes, Officer Houston walks over to me and tells me that he overheard the higher-ups talking about not wasting time on the situation, to give the man one opportunity to end the situation or they were going in, no matter the outcome.

I talk them into letting me call Dee again. I don't know if I can, but I want to talk some sense into Mark before he gets everyone inside killed. He answers on the first ring.

"Hello, Mark?"

"Say what you have to say," he says.

"Well, uhh…have you looked out your window lately?"

"I see, I see. Why'd you have to call the police?"

"Because Mark, I think something's going on inside. Where's Dee, the girls and Sean?"

Mark doesn't answer.

"Listen, Mark, I don't think this is a good thing for you to do." I don't know what else to say and I am handed a note from the officer. "Okay, Mark. Do you think you can let everyone go?"

"Let everyone go?"

"Umm, yeah, you think you can do that?"

"I found the cameras, Lala. Dee, for some crazy reason, thought I should know they were in the house after it happened again."

"It 'happened again'?"

Mark laughs. "Yes, over and over again. Maybe the next time you'll be here. How 'bout that. Lorenzo kind of told me how you like it."

I want to call him a bastard so badly. "Okay, okay, Mark. I'm asking you again. Do you think you can let everyone go and this can end peacefully?"

There is a long pause, then he says, "It's too late."

As soon as the officers hear his answer, they huddle up. I know it's just a matter of time before they are going to take matters into their own hands. I put the phone down and go back to my corner, put my face in my hands, and begin to pray.

The SWAT team decides not to move in right away. I am still in my corner and with everything going on, I am fighting sleep like never before. It's kind of chilly and it's close to one in the morning. Officer Houston drapes his jacket around my shoulders and gives me coffee. Everyone freezes for a brief second at the sound of gunshots going off inside the house. The trailer empties out in seconds; everyone storms the house to see what has happened. I run out of the trailer and stand right next to the iron steps that are anchored into the ground looking through the fog that the rain has left for the night.

When I see the girls and Sean running out of the house, then an officer placing a blanket around Dee and the dog near her side, my eyes light up and I run out into the street to greet them all with open arms. I find out later from Dee, that once Mark fell asleep, she snatched his gun out of his hand, then unloaded the entire 9mm pistol inside his body and never looked back.

Chapter 55

Two months later, I find out that our show is number one in the ratings. The company decides to throw us a party and I invite Dee, the girls, Sean, and Sydney.

The day is like no other. Not more than eighty-two degrees, not a cloud in the sky, and plenty of fun and games for the three hundred or so guests that have filled a private section of Six Flags.

I am watching Sydney, as all the grown folk sit around at a picnic table. I think I see him crack a smile. I swear, it's the first one to cover his face since we lost Nancy.

We still manage to talk and have a drink now and then. But he's still a hurt man, still regretting the words that never came out of his mouth. He still watches over me like a father, which I enjoy. I keep pushing him to relax more, but more often than I like to hear from Sydney, his street life and cronies are becoming more and more a part of his life. And I worry about him. But today, I am just happy to see him smile and relax.

❖❖❖

Dee is overjoyed with her new life. She has the nerve to be wearing a two-piece and sitting at the table with a humongous water gun on her lap for Sean the next time he appears in her sight. After pulling the trigger on Mark and freeing herself and the kids from any more harm, she has a new outlook on life. She's working out more and drinks only on special occasions. She has enough to deal with as the girls are growing up faster than she ever expected, and that boy Sean is looking more like Denzel Washington to us all every day.

I'm okay this day, too. I've pledged never to be so naïve again about anything. I have completely gotten over Keith, Adria, and their baby. But I doubt if I will ever let them know. Lorenzo is far removed from my mind as well. As I sit and talk with a producer on how we can make the show better and better for the next season, for the second time this day, my eyes run across a gorgeous man who's across the way at what seems to be his own company picnic. I can't believe that he notices my glances, then comes over to say hello.

I play his game and tell him my name.

I get his as well.

He seems nice and he's sure nuff eye candy for the soul. But as he asks if I would ever be interested in going out, I think about his offer and turn him down gently. This sista has felt enough pain for a lifetime. Plus, I am already surrounded by everyone who gives me joy. I am truly happy with that. Truly, indeed.

ABOUT THE AUTHOR

Franklin White is the author of the national bestsellers *Potentially Yours*, *Money For Good*, *Fed Up with the Fanny*, *Cup of Love* and *'Til Death Do Us Part*, a short story collection nominated for a Gold Pen Award. He is the former features editor for *Upscale* magazine as well as the writer of the column "Author2Author." He is an inductee of the Archie Givens Collection at the University of Minnesota. Franklin White is also publisher of Blue/Black Press and has worked on such notable titles as *No Matter What* with Bridgett Stewart, the upcoming *The Last Good Kiss* by Janice Pinnock, and *Playing With the Hand I Was Dealt* by Nikki Jenkins.

Visit www.franklin-white.com to learn more.